K*SS HAPPENS

JANE LYNNE DANIELS

www.BOROUGHSPUBLISHINGGROUP.com

PUBLISHER'S NOTE: This is a work of fiction. Names, characters, places and incidents either are the product of the author's imagination or are used fictitiously. Any resemblance to actual events, locales, business establishments or persons, living or dead, is coincidental. Boroughs Publishing Group does not have any control over and does not assume responsibility for author or third-party websites, blogs or critiques or their content.

K*SS HAPPENS
Copyright © 2014 Dawn Gothro

ISBN 978-1-941260-8-38

For my husband

ACKNOWLEDGMENTS

With many thanks to my wonderful and supportive editor, Jill Limber, and my critique partner, bestselling author Jami Davenport.

CONTENTS

K*SS HAPPENS

CHAPTER ONE

It was the song. The fucking song.

Its opening notes slammed Chase head-on into a memory he thought he'd left behind a long time ago.

He hadn't seen his songwriting partner, Zoe, pull the CD from the box she'd been rummaging through. Hadn't looked up when she'd asked, "What's this?" If he had, he might have realized what she held in her hand before she stuck it in a player and the sound of his guitar, followed by Emma's voice, crashed through the room and into his head.

He spun on his boot heel and hurled a snarl at Zoe. "What the *hell* do you think you're doing?"

Her jaw dropped. For the first time since he'd known her, she appeared speechless.

Chase felt like shit for yelling at her, even as he fought the images of Emma's face and the scent of lavender and Dial soap, tucked into the soft corner of her neck that rocketed through him.

He didn't need this, not now. He didn't know where Emma was and he didn't want to. Some things needed to be left the fuck alone.

On the CD, Emma's voice turned breathless. In 5.3 seconds, Chase's would join hers on the recording, their voices melding, strengthening, rising—

His boots rang out on the wood floor as he crossed the room to switch off the player and punch the eject button. He sent the CD sailing across the room like a silver Frisbee. It clattered on the floor.

Silence while Zoe looked him over. Then she drawled, "Somethin' wrong, Chap*man*?"

He hated when she did that to his last name. And she knew it. But then no one talked like he just had to Zoe Webb. The woman had a Grammy for co-writing a song of the year. A Grammy caked with blood from all the people she'd knocked in the head to get where she was.

He raked a hand through his hair and answered, without moving his mouth, "We're done for today."

"Like hell we are."

A ray of sunlight through the window caught the CD. It winked up at him from the floor. "Just go."

"This place isn't ready for a photo shoot." She glanced around at the boxes that were still unopened. "Not one with me in it, anyway."

People magazine was coming to his new house tomorrow to take pictures for an article on country music's hottest songwriting duo. This followed a spread a few months ago in *That's Country* magazine. Chase could do without the publicity, but Zoe ate it up.

"Anything still in a box, I'll shove in a closet." *Just leave me alone.*

Zoe's whistle, low and sarcastic, scraped against the edges of his one nerve not under assault. "So who is she?"

"Go. Please." Only that last nerve could manage to make it a request.

"Uh-*huh*." Zoe exaggerated her southern accent, which showed up when it suited her to be southern. "Hometown sweetheart. That's it, isn't it? Miss What's-it-County Apple Queen. Did you use your guitar to get her into the backseat of your car? Sing to her all nice and easy?"

"Get. Out."

"We could do something with that, you know." She pulled a melody out of the air to sing in her raspy bourbon-and-violets voice, "Just him and a beat-up old *guitar* in the back of my daddy's *car*." She paused, squinting at a spot somewhere past him. "Too bad it's been done about a million times already."

"Shut. *Up*." He took her arm to pull her toward the door.

"Oooh. Hit a nerve." Zoe's gaze narrowed as he pulled the door open. "Maybe I *do* smell a hit song comin' on."

He moved his hand from her arm to her back, pushing her forward. The heavy wooden door groaned when he opened it.

She blew him a kiss, gave him the finger, and ducked outside right before he slammed the door.

Chase leaned up against it and closed his eyes. There'd be hell to pay with Zoe tomorrow. For once, he didn't care.

This time when his boots hit the floor, his steps were determined, deliberate. For the tenth or one hundred and tenth time over the last several years—he'd lost count—he picked up his guitar, gripped it hard in his hands and tried to exorcise Emma's hold on him the only way he knew how.

Finish the song they'd started together.

The damn, fucking song.

***

Emma Zane pulled the collar of her coat tight and gripped the handle of her umbrella until her fingers felt numb. A large raindrop wiggled along the fabric's edge at eye level, distorting the words of a sign reading: *Madame Claire, Psychic. Predictions with a 95% success rate.*

She shook the raindrop free, watching it splash to the pavement. Then she sidestepped the puddle it joined. A laid-off music teacher couldn't afford to ruin her shoes. Or to come down with pneumonia because of wet feet.

Not to mention a laid-off music teacher who had not found another job despite doing everything short of begging for one and who had burned through her sacred emergency fund just to keep a roof over her head. When funds tightened, middle school music programs were expendable. And Emma wasn't qualified for much else. Not that anyone in Seattle was hiring for much else.

She hoped the soulless number crunchers were happy when this generation of kids grew up craving the music that would feed and validate their emotional ups and downs, without having the first idea how to make it.

Her eyes followed the arrow on the sign, looking up at the stairs leading to the psychic's place. This was crazy. *So* crazy.

But she'd promised her new friend Tensley she'd come. The bookstore owner had been kind when Emma had broken down in the shop, letting things spill out of her mouth that had been bottled up inside her for too long. The cork had popped without warning.

Tensley had taken her to a back room, given her tissues to dry her tears. And listened. Sympathetically and without judgment. After several minutes, Tensley stood and began to pace, her arms hugging her middle, her mouth pressed into a line.

Emma had stopped talking and swiped at her tears. Had she shared too much? Overstepped the friendship line? Cheeks flaming, Emma picked up her purse, ready to make her escape.

Her friend's brows had drawn together in a fierce V. "There's someone I want you to see."

"Th-thank you, but—" Emma had fumbled for the right response. "I don't need a therapist. Just having you listen helped." She waved a hand. "Don't worry about me. I'll be fi—" She'd hiccupped and put her hand to her mouth. "Fine."

"I'm serious. You need to see her. She's a, you know, a person who can—" Tensley had put her hands on her hips and shook her head, opening and closing her mouth several times before admitting, "Okay, she's a psychic. And she's gotten a few things wrong in the past, but she's promised me she has it all figured out now."

A psychic. Really? As in 1-800-I'll-tell-you-what-you-want-to-hear? That was sweet of Tensley, in a misguided kind of way. Emma drew her shoulders back and breathed in deep, trying to decide how to thank her friend without hurting her feelings.

With a sharp nod, Tensley said, "I'm calling her right now."

"Wait!" Emma didn't need a psychic; she needed a job. A life. A memory chip she could erase. "Don't. Please. I'm sorry I bothered you. Just having a bad day, I guess." She put a hand to her temple and gave Tensley a duh-silly-me look. "I don't even know where all of that came from. Forget about it. Please." She stumbled over her own feet as she rose and had to grip the arm of the chair to keep from falling. "But thank you for listening."

"Sit."

Emma stopped, still holding on to the chair, not sure what to do next.

"Trust me," Tensley said.

That was the point. Emma didn't do trust. But she sat, because she couldn't be impolite. Her mother had raised her better than that.

She crossed and uncrossed her fingers, wishing she could press a rewind button as Tensley left the room to make the call. Emma heard her raise her voice, caught a few of her words. "Don't screw things up again," Tensley said into the phone.

Again Emma straightened. She should leave now. There were other bookstores she could go to. She'd never have to come back here again, never have to face someone who had heard all about the things she never told anyone.

Tensley returned, her expression grim. She held out a piece of paper. "This is the address. Promise me you'll go. She's expecting you."

"I don't know why I got so upset, but I'm fine now. You don't have to worry about me."

"*Promise.*"

"I—" What, had anything else to do?

"Things will change after you see her."

"About time." Emma tried a laugh, but it twisted into a strangled half cough. She looked at her feet, twisting the strap of her purse. "Okay. I guess. I mean, thanks." She glanced up, but looked away when she saw the sympathy in her friend's eyes.

There was a reason she didn't open up like she just had. Genuine sympathy was harder to take than the everyday "How are you?" between work friends that really meant *Tell me anything else.* Sympathy made Emma feel exposed and if not broken, at least bent. What the hell had been wrong with her, telling Tensley all of that?

"Don't thank me," Tensley had said. "Go see her now and then just…have a good life."

Have a good life. As in, don't ever come back here again and cry all over my counter and K-cups. Could there be anyone more pitiful than Emma Zane? Couldn't even keep her feelings inside, where they belonged.

Tensley waited. Emma gulped and mumbled, "Of course." Then she left. Or, more accurately, fled.

She'd gone straight to the address on the paper because one, she didn't break promises, and two, it seemed the least she could do for being such a sobbing loser mess.

Get it over with, she told herself. *How bad can it be?*

She went up the stairs until she reached the door and pushed it open. Overhead, bells jingled.

The room was small, lit by candles and a small lamp. Incense, spiraling in curls from a burner on the top of a black table, clung to the air. An overstuffed sofa in one corner held so many pillows, its seat cushions had all but disappeared.

A squeak of wood and a door in the back of the room opened. An older woman, dressed in black, her ankles wobbling in leopard-print heels, stepped out. Stripes of gray ran along both sides of the part in her dark hair. And on her lips, she wore a bright red lipstick that caused her pale skin to fade in defeat. "Ah," she said. "So you have come."

Emma peered closer. The statement was confident, but she could feel doubt emanating from the woman's small frame.

"You are the friend." A pause. "Is that not true?"

An odd accent wove through the woman's words. It seemed to start out in northern Europe and turn south at Tennessee before making its way toward Russia. Emma took a step backward.

"I'm…" *Wishing I wasn't here.*

"Ee-mah," the woman said.

It took Emma a few seconds to recognize her name. "Yes. That's, uh, me. You're Madame Claire?"

"Indeed." The woman nodded. "I have been waiting for you." She took a step to one side and motioned Emma forward, into the other room.

Emma peered into it, looking for an emergency exit. Just in case.

Madame Claire clasped her hands together. "It is not all day I have."

She looked nervous, which made Emma even more nervous. "I can come back another time," Emma offered.

The psychic's tight expression said otherwise.

"Okay," Emma whispered. She did as she'd been told. As she walked by the other woman, she could have sworn she smelled alcohol hovering beneath the incense. *Great. A psychic guilty of Reading under the Influence.*

The room was small, lit only by a glass lamp with dangling crystals. The kind of lamp Hollywood put in the whorehouses of movies set in the old West. A pocket-sized fan blew a small breeze that had the crystals tinkling as they bumped into each other.

Madame Claire motioned Emma to sit opposite her at a small table. Emma took her seat, the wood pressing into her bony butt, which was about to get a whole lot bonier if she didn't start making money again soon.

The psychic closed her eyes and bent her head. Then she opened her eyes and reached across the table to take Emma's hands in hers. Emma could feel the woman's fingers trembling.

"You have a deep regret," said Madame Claire. Her voice was measured, as though she recited the words from a memorized script.

Emma's jaw dropped as a sliver of dread made its way from her heart to her brain. She knew. This woman knew things.

No. She *couldn't*. Everybody knew psychics started off with something that could broadly apply. Most people carried some kind of regret.

Emma cleared her throat. "Go on," she said, dragging out the two syllables in the way she imagined a calm, in-control person might do.

"This regret; it is about a man."

Emma shook her head. *Yes, it is. No, it isn't.*

The dark eyes that met hers appeared confused at first, then curious. "No," Madame Claire said slowly, "It is more about the...how do you say it, the opportunity. The one you did not take."

Ha. Now she got it. Tensley had filled the woman in, maybe because she thought Emma needed to hear that everything would be okay from a disinterested third party. Disinterested in everything but money, that is. "You've been talking with my friend."

Madame Claire's gaze turned piercing. "It is music I hear."

"Um...what?"

"You wrote words to this music. With this man." She began to hum, a little off-tune, but the notes, the melody, it was—

Oh shit. It couldn't be. This woman couldn't possibly know.

Emma scrawled words on her mental chalkboard and quickly erased them, the dust flying, all over her hands, onto her black shoes. A psychic could not, would not, read her mind.

And then she did. "My...lonesome...my..."

No, no, no. In her brain, one hand wrote the next word faster than the other hand could send it into chalk dust.

"Wish...some..."

Emma's stomach formed a giant knot, sending distress signals through her. She wrenched her hands away to clutch at her stomach, pressing her index finger hard against her rib, as though pain somewhere else could stop the pain she didn't want to think about.

"What does this mean, this wish some?"

"Stop," Emma choked out. This woman couldn't know those words, couldn't be saying them. Emma hadn't told Tensley anything about the song. The fucking song.

"Why you did not go with him?" Madame Claire asked.

She wrote *scared* on her mental board, pressing so hard the white chalk snapped in half, sending dust scattering and falling through the air.

The psychic nodded, as if Emma had answered. "This then, is your deepest regret. That you could not believe."

Emma bowed her head. She pulled her hands away from her stomach to stare at her fingers, flexing them while noting that the polish on one fingernail had chipped. The others would begin to go any minute, she suspected. It summed things up, after all. A bottle of Sing Me Crazy Red, bright and shiny at first, then peeling away, bit by bit, to reveal the vanilla-nothing nails beneath, chewed at the edges.

Nothing lasts. Especially bright and shiny things.

"This regret," the psychic went on, "it has worn a hole inside and there is—" Her hands flailed in the air. "What do I mean to say, there is…ahhhh, *bitterness* that leaks into every part of you." Satisfied with her ability to make this pronouncement, she folded her arms on the table, watching Emma with an expectant gaze.

A spark fired within her. "That's not true." In an instant, she flashed back to her principal, to his startled expression when Emma had called the language arts teacher who got to stay a "clock-watcher with a Dickens-size stick up her ass." And then dissolved into apologies. So bitterness leaked. Who knew.

"There were things you did not understand at the time."

She'd understood everything and nothing. But more than anything, she'd wanted Chase to think that what they had together was enough, to understand that taking foolish risks was just that. Foolish. To understand that, after growing up with a mother who kept going back to the broken promises buffet for more, Emma hated taking chances.

She'd been so tempted, though. There had never been anyone like Chase, never anyone but him for her. She couldn't look into his eyes without seeing into his rough, gentle, and fiery soul. Couldn't brush against him without longing to feel his arms, strong, warm, and pulsing with life, wrap around her and carry her to his bed.

Something was leaking, all right, but it wasn't bitterness. At the thought of Chase, Emma's eyes had become wet, her panties damp, and she was breaking into a sweat.

"That's enough," she whispered, but her voice lifted on the last word in a question she didn't, couldn't mean. She folded her arms around herself and tried again. "It's not as though I can do anything about it now."

Madame Claire hesitated before answering, "True in your world. Not so in mine."

Emma didn't know what that meant. She wanted to make herself as small as she could and slink out of the room. Maybe the psychic wouldn't notice. A lot of people didn't. Not anymore.

"Tell me please. If you could have a do-over," Madame Claire said, pronouncing the term as though she had to roll it around her mouth like a marble, "what would it be?"

"I can't." An ocean of sadness swept over her.

"But you can. One."

"One."

"One."

"A do-over."

The other woman gestured toward her ear. "Trouble with the hearing? I said you can have one. What is it to be?"

Okay, then. Emma would play along, if only to get out of this place as fast as she could. She straightened, summoning her teacher voice, the one that made eleven-year-olds in the back row stop tormenting their friends long enough to pay attention. "Fine. If I had a do-over, I would have gone to Nashville with Chase."

For just a second, for one second, it felt as though, by admitting her biggest regret, she'd at least applied a Band-Aid to it. The kind with antibiotic. *Huh.* She sat back against the chair, the wooden slats pressing hard into her. So Tensley had given her a dose of psychic therapy, which might not be so bad, after all.

Too late to do any good, but not so bad.

Madame Claire watched her closely. "If this is what you choose, then it shall be so."

A reality check might be in order. "Or as *so* as anything is."

"When you leave this place, you will have done as you wished. But remember, this will only happen once."

"Ri-i-ght." Emma was beginning to wonder what sort of delusional psychics Tensley hung around. It was one thing to play with an idea, another to pronounce it as fact.

"Your friend Tensley, it was the same with her, though it nearly all turned out badly. She came back." Madame Claire shook her head. "She should not have done so." She leaned across the table. "You must not do that. Make your promise."

"I'm not sure what you—"

"Make your promise!"

"Okay. Sure." Emma put up a hand. "I promise not to come back." That was an easy one.

"Good." Madame Claire appeared satisfied. "Your friend, she has paid for this session, so you may leave." Her words were an abrupt dismissal.

Emma shot up from the chair, eager to go. Eager to keep herself from thinking about what would have happened had she really gone to Nashville.

"Stop!"

Emma turned.

"One more thing," the woman thundered. "You are to tell no one."

"Of course. I mean, no. I won't." Tell them what exactly?

"You must not take this lightly. Tell anyone and all will unravel most unpredictably. There will be nothing I can do. You understand?"

Absolutely not. "Yes."

"You will go now."

Well, fine. She didn't want to stay. Emma walked out of the room so quickly she tripped over her shoes, but she recovered in time to prevent a face plant on the hardwood floor. "Thank you," she called over one shoulder, pretty sure she didn't mean it.

At the last minute, as she wrapped her hand around the doorknob, the metal cold on her skin, something made her look back.

She saw the psychic raise her arms slowly in the air, her lips moving. A white light flashed over her head, raining a shower of sparks down upon her. Emma froze. She opened her mouth to ask if the woman was okay, if she'd been caught in…an indoor electrical storm? But then she heard Madame Claire's voice, clear and strong.

"You. Will. Get. Out. Of. Here!"

Emma fled. Straight out the door.

And on to some sort of a stage, with lights that hurt her eyes. Another woman stood next to her, the cloying scent of her hair spray stinging Emma's nostrils.

"What the—?" Emma lifted a hand to shade her eyes as a harsh white spotlight trained on her. Applause rang in her ears and she looked down to see that the cold object gripped in her other hand was actually a crystal trophy. In the shape of a chart bullet. With a bronze medallion. Even a person in her not-right mind, as Emma seemed to be, would recognize it as a Country Music Association award.

In *her* hand.

Beads from Emma's dress caught the light and sparkled up at her. She closed her eyes in slow motion, waiting for the paramedics to load her onto the stretcher. This must be what a breakdown felt like.

She hoped someone would remember to feed her cat. While she was locked away.

CHAPTER TWO

Emma felt the sharp point of an elbow in her ribs. *"Hon-n-ney,"* said a female voice in a stage whisper caught by the microphone. "Y'all can feel free to leave the stage now."

Good-natured laughter rippled through the room, wrapping around Emma like a fuzzy blanket. She opened her eyes to an auditorium filled with people dressed in everything from formal gowns to blue jeans with cowboy hats, all eyes trained on her. *Her.*

Her gaze swept to her fingers, tipped in perfect Sing Me Crazy Red polish, gripping the crystal trophy so hard her knuckles had turned white.

Again with the elbow in her ribs. She glanced over to see an older woman at her side, a smile straining the edges of her Botoxed face. The woman pressed icy fingertips into the bare skin of Emma's arm. "Move it, sister," she whispered, away from the microphone this time. "You're not the only one who's ever written a song."

Written a song. The CMAs. Could this be the moment she'd dreamed of as a teenager who longed to write songs other people would want to perform?

"Song of the Year?" she whispered to the woman, half-expecting her to laugh at the audacity of the question. *Are you kidding me, the most prestigious award given to a songwriter?*

"Sure is," the woman said between clenched teeth, still smiling.

Wow. As Disney said, dreams really do come true. Emma lifted her hand in a shy wave to the crowd.

Music began to play and the Queen of Botox, tip-tapping on wobbly heels with the speed of a deranged hummingbird, pulled her toward the wings.

"Hey," Emma protested, lifting the hem of her skirt so she wouldn't trip, which—if this really *was* the CMAs—would make for a photo she'd see splashed across *Entertainment Tonight*. *Ha.* Her. On *ET*. She half-snorted, half-giggled.

The gown was feathery light, with thousands, or at least hundreds, of tiny hundred-watt beads catching the lights. She felt like Glinda, the Good Country Witch. The fabric didn't even have weight in her hands. She hoped she had a good bra on because this thing had to be transparent.

"Don't worry. I've got her," drawled a deep voice from her other side. She looked up to see a tall, handsome man in a white cowboy hat grinning down at her. He too held a crystal CMA award, but he shifted it to his other hand so he could grip her elbow. His skin was warm on hers. He looked familiar.

With an irritated toss of her hair extensions, the older woman released her cold hands from Emma's arm and scurried into one of the curtained hallways backstage.

"We did it," said the man beside Emma. When she turned, he leaned down to plant a kiss on her lips. Before Emma could find her voice, he winked and said, "See ya in a minute." Emma stared after him, realizing why he looked familiar. It was Jason Jeffries, a rising country music star she'd seen profiled only last week. On *ET*.

As quickly as he strode away, another woman, gripping a jeweled handbag and a notebook, invaded Emma's personal space. "Congratulations, Ms. Zane!" she squeaked, her face alight. "So deserved, so well deserved."

"Thank you," Emma said, taking a step backward.

The perky woman lowered her voice. "I can't believe Etta Dorcas would speak that way to you. She's just jealous, that's all."

Etta Dorcas? As in, the songwriter of five straight number-one country hits when Emma was in middle school? "Don't say that. Etta Dorcas is a legend."

The other woman's nostrils pinched, in apparent confusion. "Um, yes, ma'am. But you said they only asked her to present the Song of the Year award because they must have a rule or something about showing respect for has-beens."

Emma blinked. "Me? I wouldn't say something like that. It's so…*rude*." She turned away, toward a passing man in a very large cowboy hat. "Why would I say that?"

With a smile, he touched his fingers to the brim of his hat and kept walking.

"Omigod," Emma breathed. She grasped the wrist of the woman at her side. "Was that who I *think* it was?"

The woman looked up and to the side, her expression perplexed, before finally asking, "Miss Zane, are you feeling all right?"

Emma pondered that. "I don't think so. But that's okay. I might be having fun for the first time in forever." Her gaze drifted to the woman's notebook, where she saw a name engraved in leather across the top. She tried it out. "Taryn."

The woman nodded in short, sharp jerks, her over-plucked brows furrowing. "As soon as you do your media time, we'll hustle you out of here to the parties, ma'am."

Emma looked around her, spotting two more ginormous country stars chatting. One turned and gave her a tight wave. All around, she felt electric anticipation in the air, heard voices over a microphone and applause coming from the auditorium.

Musicians holding guitars made their way past her to the stage. It was all Emma could do to keep from squealing like a teenager at the excitement of it all. "Are you kidding?" she asked Taryn. "Why would I want to leave this?"

The other woman's lashes went into a rapid blink-fest. "The after-parties, ma'am. But only the ones you said you wanted to go to. I know I'm new and as you said, you have no reason to have confidence in me, but I assure you I took care of everything. Limos, your dress, all of it. Exactly as instructed."

Emma shook her head and craned her neck to see if she could tell which musicians were speaking. All of her favorites had to be here. Live and in person. At the *CMAs*. "I'm sure you did," she murmured, distracted.

"I should have anticipated you would want to stay longer. Of course."

Emma turned back to see Taryn drop the notebook to her side with a thump, her face crumpling before she pulled her mouth tight. "What's wrong?" Emma asked, concerned.

"I'm doing my best, ma'am."

"Of course. I'm sure you are. At…what you do."

Unshed tears glimmered in Taryn's eyes, but she straightened and squared her shoulders. "I'll make different arrangements."

"It's okay. I'll do whatever you tell me to." This dream couldn't last that much longer, anyway.

"Oh no, ma'am. I would never presume to tell you what to do."

"Please don't call me ma'am. It makes me feel like I should be knitting you a sweater."

"But you told me to."

"I *didn't*—" Emma stopped. "I mean—Call me Emma. Please."

Taryn drew a breath and tipped her head, apparently doing her best to regroup. "Would you like to go over the itinerary again?"

Would she? Emma had no idea. "There's an itinerary?"

"Yes, ma'am. Um—Miss Zane. Maybe you should look it over before you talk with the media. I'll get you a glass of water." She consulted her notebook. "Three cubes of ice and two slices of lemon. Got it."

Emma put her hands to the sides of her head. What the hell was going on? "I'd prefer something a lot stronger than water. And I should sit down."

Taryn scooted across the floor to grab a chair. "Here you are."

Emma sank into it, grateful for the feeling of something solid beneath her. Her knees had begun to shake, causing the beads of the gown to dance in the muted lights. "What am I doing here?" She folded her arms around her middle, beaded fabric pressing into her skin.

"I'll be right back." Taryn disappeared, returning a few minutes later to press a glass of water on Emma.

She stared at it. Three cubes of ice and two lemon slices. She took a long, cool drink. It helped.

The other woman knelt beside her. After a minute, she said, "I don't mean to push you, ma'am, but they're waiting for you."

"Who?"

"The media."

"Why?"

"They talk with all of the winners." Taryn's voice quavered. "And it's your turn."

Emma worked her mouth for a few seconds before summoning the courage to ask, "What did I win for?"

That question appeared to tip Taryn further toward the edge. She gaped at Emma. "Song of the Year. Ma'am."

"Song of the Year?" Emma screeched. A man in a black cowboy hat frowned at her from beneath its brim.

"Okay, we can deal with this," Taryn said to the floor, as if it were only her and the wooden boards having a conversation. "I can say she's not feeling well, she has food poisoning, it kicked in as soon as she left the stage, she's in the bathroom, she's throwing up, she can't possibly meet with the media. No. Not throwing up. Too messy. Especially in that dress, which has to be returned. A fever.

That's it. Coming down with something. Probably contagious. No one should be around her."

"What are you talking about?"

"She doesn't want to get anyone else sick…" Taryn looked up, mid-rambling. "Sorry, ma'am, just trying to think how to get you out of here."

Not so fast. "Where do I go?"

Taryn blinked. "What?"

"To talk to the media. Where do I go?" No reason to waste this gorgeous dress, when it could be featured in fake photos. Emma stood up, feeling ridiculously refreshed and once again enjoying the swirling beads as the fabric fell into place.

"Are you sure you—"

"Positive."

Taryn bit her lip and re-squared her shoulders. "Of course. Right this way," she said.

The media area was smaller than it looked on TV and packed with a whirlwind of activity. Emma stood in front of the background with the CMA logo and smiled her brightest, wincing at the rapid-fire camera flashes.

"How does it feel to win Song of the Year?" called one reporter.

"Amazing," Emma responded, just as she remembered hearing other artists respond to similar questions. She only wished she knew what song had allegedly won. And she wished she knew where the hell Chase was. Why wasn't he up here with her? What an inconsiderate dreamer she was not to include him.

She cast a glance to the side, hoping to see him. This was everything they'd ever hoped for. Once upon a time.

A man in a crisp shirt with a headset gestured her to move along. A glance to her other side and she saw Jason Jeffries striding toward her, his award cupped in one hand. He grinned.

"Jason," another reporter called. "How long did it take you two to write 'Wishsome'?"

Emma froze. "What?" she managed.

Jason Jeffries put an arm around her waist. She straight-armed him and the camera flashes went off again. "What did you say?" she asked the reporter again.

The reporter, his slicked-back blond hair like icing on a tanned cake, perked up. "'Wishsome.' Song of the Year. How long did it take you to write it?"

"But we never finished it." She was confused. Very confused.

Taryn materialized out of nowhere. "*Ma'am. This way.*"

Emma's feet wouldn't move. "Where's Chase?" she asked the reporter, since he seemed to be the only one not trying to hustle her away.

Taryn sidled closer. "Ms. Zane," she whispered.

"Chase who?" the reporter shot back.

The guy with the headset jammed his hands on his waist, making it clear he expected to be obeyed. Jason Jeffries flashed his pearly caps.

"Chase Chapman," Emma said. He should be by her side. They had won Song of the Year for "Wishsome." Her heart began to soar at the thought, but was smashed back to ground level by the next reporter's question.

"How does it feel to win for writing your first number one hit, Jason?"

Jason Jeffries didn't write "Wishsome." He *didn't*. He might have sung it, which, okay, would be pretty amazing, but he did not write it.

"Aw now, Emma's the one most responsible for that," he drawled. "She's the one who writes the words. I'm just a plain old picker. Not hard to write a melody when you have lyrics like that."

"Seriously?" Emma turned to the handsome, whisker-stubbled face of the singer, who moved his arm upward to drape it around her bare shoulders. This close, he looked a little too perfect. Not a single crease in his jeans and not so much as a speck of dust on his white cowboy hat. Highly suspicious.

More camera flashes. He smiled down at her and she had the distinct impression he wasn't even seeing her; he was instead positioning his face for the most advantageous camera angle.

"How does it feel being one of the hottest couples in country music?" asked another reporter.

Jason didn't take his eyes off Emma. "I feel lucky she'll have me," he said, his breath tickling her nose. "We make beautiful music together."

"If that's the best you can do, it's a good thing you don't write lyrics, Jason," someone laughed.

His eyes narrowed so briefly, Emma was sure she was the only one who caught it. Then he was back to his charming self. "Now guys, that hurts," he said with a laugh. He dropped a kiss on Emma's head and ever-so-slightly nudged her with his hip. Taryn did the rest, pulling her away so Jason could continue flashing his smile and fielding questions.

"I want to know where Chase is," Emma said as Taryn led them down a winding hallway.

"I'm sorry; I don't know who that is."

"He co-wrote "Wishsome"!" She didn't mean to scream it, but it felt as though there were a hundred tiny voices of alarm all clamoring at the same time and no one but her could hear them.

Taryn pulled to a stop, nearly causing a hallway pileup. *"Ma-am,"* she whispered.

"I said not to call me that."

Once again, rapid blinking in response. "Miss Zane," Taryn said, her voice losing none of its urgency. "You do not want to say something like that. You and Jason Jeffries wrote that song. His label wouldn't want you saying someone else was involved. Someone who didn't get credit."

Emma shook her head, trying to understand. She pinched herself on the wrist. Hard. *Ow.* "Am I really here?"

"Yes, ma'am, I mean—Miss Zane. You are. After a lot of hard work."

Emma aimed a suspicious look at her. "You said you were new. How do you know?"

"Full briefing from your previous assistant."

An assistant. She had an assistant. And the pinch hadn't awakened her, so maybe this *wasn't* a dream. The psychic. Her second chance. The do-over. Those white sparks above Madame Claire's head.

It was insane, impossible. *What had happened to Chase?*

"I'm not perfect, but I don't lie," Emma said, feeling anxiety crease her face. "Chase co-wrote that song."

Silence as her assistant looked at her, possibly listening for the first time.

After a moment, Taryn said, "Then that's something you'll want to keep to yourself."

"I can't. It's not right."

"There's a lot that isn't right about this business. But you haven't come this far to let it all be taken away from you now." Taryn's mouth snapped shut, as though she realized she'd gone too far. Her cheeks pinked.

Emma chose her next words carefully. "I understand. I think." What had she gotten herself into?

Taryn urged her forward. "We need to get you changed for the party."

"One more thing."

"Of course."

"Jason Jeffries…" She didn't know how to ask without sounding like an idiot.

"He's going in a different car, but will meet you there."

"Why?"

Taryn consulted her paperwork. "That's what his publicist said. You'll arrive at the same time, though."

"No. I mean, why am I going with him?"

"Why?" Taryn's confidence seemed to leave her body and float past, out of her grasp. "Because, um, that's what you do when you're dating. Ma'am."

"Dating," Emma repeated. She was dating a country star.

"And we're all set to coordinate the announcement with his publicist. When you're ready."

"Announcement." Emma shook her head. "I'm not sure what you mean."

Taryn glanced furtively to each side and then tapped the third finger of her left hand. "*That* announcement. No reason for every woman in Nashville to hate you before it's necessary."

Understanding dawned. "Engagement announcement," Emma said, unwilling to believe it. "I'm going to marry him."

"Yes, ma'am."

So she hadn't found Chase, but she apparently *had* pledged her undying love to a country star who ironed his jeans, wore more makeup than she did, and spoke in clichés.

Now there was a "do-over" for you.

CHAPTER THREE

Chase surveyed the damage to his grandfather's barn. With the cold, calculating and guilty gaze of the one who had caused it.

Because of the song. The damn, fucking song.

He didn't listen to contemporary country any more. He liked the classics—Waylon, Johnny, George. They were his brothers in arms, the ones who knew about betrayal in all its forms, and sang about it. Which was pretty much all Chase himself sang about these days. To his audience of one, Lila, a yellow Lab he'd adopted from the Humane Society.

Still, he'd been playing backup some nights for the band of a guy he'd met at the local Moonshine Festival and once they'd finished the set last night, he'd stuck around for beers. Not long after, a shit-ass version of "Wishsome" had begun playing on the satellite radio station in the club.

It wasn't the melody that got him. It only vaguely resembled the one he'd written years ago and it was nothing special. Anyone schooled in the pop shit that passed for country now could have written it.

No. It had been the words. Emma's unmistakable lyrics. He'd choked on his beer when he heard them and sputtered, "What the *hell*?"

His new buddy Carl, sitting on the barstool next to him, turned to say, "Hey, you don't like the beer, I'll take it."

Chase slammed the bottle to the counter. "That *song*. What the fuck is it?"

"Man, you don't get out much. That song's all over the place." Carl flinched under Chase's glare. "'Wishsome.' Big hit for Jason Jeffries."

A red-hot fury had started from a place deep inside Chase and risen until it clouded his vision, obliterated his thoughts. Jason Jeffries. Of course it was. First the fucking plastic cowboy takes Emma; then he takes their song.

He strode out of the bar so fast, so hard, he had only a vague impression of people scattering to get out of his way. Somehow he'd driven back to the house, truck tires spinning dirt and gravel when he pulled up in front. Then he'd found the bourbon and started pouring.

This morning, he didn't remember a lot else. Just the strangely pleasant sensation of taking an axe to the cabinets he'd worked so hard to build and sand, prepping them to be stained today.

The southern Ohio sun streamed through a gap in the barn's wooden boards, illuminating the pile of wrecked wood at its center. Lila sat on the other side, her tail still for once. She watched him with concerned dog eyes, waiting for a sign that her person was okay.

He gave her half a shrug. Clearly, he wasn't.

Lila padded to his side and he reached down to let his fingers linger on her soft furry head as he continued to assess the state of things. The house and barn had stood empty since his grandfather died ten years ago. Chase's parents had agreed to let him live here, in exchange for fixing the place up, after Chase had aimlessly bounced around playing clubs for a couple of years until he'd run out of money.

He'd put days into building those cabinets and it had probably taken only a few minutes to destroy them.

All because of a memory he *couldn't* destroy, no matter how hard he tried.

He kicked at the splintered wood with the dusty toe of one boot. The cabinets had been meant to go in the room he'd chosen for writing the music that continued to pulse through his veins. Some days he toyed with the idea of bringing Emma here to repair their relationship, which had meant more to him than anything before, ever, in his whole life. Other days, he knew what a crock of shit that idea was.

She was a success now. He wasn't.

"Mornin'."

Chase spun around and suffered the consequences of a still-woozy head. He stopped himself from falling by grabbing the side of a rusty riding lawnmower. Straightening, he answered Carl. "Good morning."

"Thought you might be a little worse for the wear today." Carl hooked his thumbs into his jeans. "Beth sent me over to check on you."

"No need. I'm good."

The other man's gaze went from Chase, still unsteady on his feet, to the pile of massacred wood, and back again. "Uh-huh.

Probably a story there, but I'm not gonna ask." He paused. "Beth might, though."

Carl's pregnant, cheerful wife had invited Chase to their house for dinner right after they all met at the Moonshine Festival and then wondered aloud which of the women in her wide circle of friends would be right for him. He'd begged off being fixed up but had known she'd be a force to be reckoned with.

"Don't tell her. Please." The wound was as fresh as if the knife had just been pulled out, leaving all of his insides exposed. He had to sew it up and slap a new bandage on it. Fast.

Carl didn't say anything for a minute as he regarded Chase. Then, "Much as it would help me to have her worry about someone else for a change, guess I don't have to tell her I found you looking like someone ran you over with your truck a few times and then poured Earl John's special batch down your throat."

Chase shook his head. Big mistake. He grimaced. "I'm fine."

"If you say so. Lemme know if you need anything." Carl turned to go then hesitated. "Does it have anything to do with that song? Shit, I thought you were about to kill somebody when it came on."

Only one somebody. Jason Jeffries. "Nah," he lied. "It just sounded familiar. That's all."

Carl climbed into his truck, staring out the windshield and then glancing back at Chase. "I'd steer clear of the radio then. Can't go more than ten minutes without hearing that song play." He closed the truck door with a bang. With a wave, he drove off.

Chase watched him disappear down the road. Lila nudged his leg, and when he looked down, she glanced back at the pile of wood as if to ask, "What now, genius?"

He wished to hell he knew the answer.

***

The after-party was held in the kind of restaurant Emma never went to, one so fancy she was sure it didn't put prices on its menu. The surroundings were softly plush and elegant, in shades of red and gray.

The food weighing down the cloth-covered tables looked like something out of a magazine shoot, the drinks were flowing, the cowboy hats were plentiful, the lights were twinkling like stars, and the air kisses were flowing.

Jason grasped Emma's fingers so hard, parts went numb as he led her through the crowded room. A blur of faces, some recognizable, others not, paraded past and congratulated them. A few raised glasses. One gave her a sudden, hard hug. Southern accents drawled over her as she and Jason did a slow-moving victory lap through the mass of sparkling gowns and dark suits.

Emma held her eyes open so wide, they began to ache. On the other side of the tight knots of people, a band started to play, the guitars waging a battle with the singers' harmonies.

She managed to slip her hand from Jason's while he was talking with a man who had raised his voice so loud to be heard over the music, it reverberated through her ears.

Making herself as small as possible, she squeezed through openings in the crowd with murmured *excuse me's* until she reached a vacant spot with breathing room. She leaned against the wall and a lanky waiter was at her side within seconds, bending to offer her champagne from the glasses on his tray.

"Oh! No, thank—" she started to say, but then changed her mind mid-sentence. "Why the hell not," she said, taking one.

"Why the hell not," he replied with a smile.

"Wait." She caught him as he began to walk away. "I'll take another, just in case." She did, holding one in each hand.

"It's best. You never know."

He seemed like a nice guy, she thought gratefully. "I don't suppose you know if there's anywhere quiet I could sit. I just need to get my thoughts together." Her thoughts, truth be told, were screaming *Run for your life!* and either frantically ramming each other in bumper cars or leaping tall buildings.

It wasn't pretty living in her head right now. A glass of champagne might help. Two glasses might help more.

"Of course," the waiter said. "Right this way." He led her to a booth built into a corner of the room, lined in rich wood paneling and lit with candles in the center of the table. "It's at least a little quieter here, and you can drop these curtains for privacy. He demonstrated by releasing one from the hook that held it back. The fabric dropped over half of the opening to the booth.

"Exactly what I need. Thank you so much." Emma fumbled with the clasp of her purse but finally got it open and reached inside to find a ten-dollar bill to hand him.

"Thank you, miss. My pleasure." And he was gone.

Emma sank into the leather cushion and closed her eyes, doing her best to take everything in and make some sense of it.

Apparently, she'd been given her do-over, as crazy as that sounded. She'd not only gone to Nashville, she'd made it to the big time. *Without Chase.* How could that have happened?

A hard plunk on the table rattled the silverware and dishes. Emma's eyes flew open to see a crystal trophy reflected in the candlelight. Her gaze swept the length of the arm that held it until it reached a large white cowboy hat and the face of the man grinning beneath its brim.

"There you are," Jason Jeffries said, removing his hat. "Hey, this thing shouldn't be down. You tryin' to hide out on our big night?" He pulled back the one side curtain that had been drawn and tucked it to the side. Before Emma could react, he gave a whoop and slid into the booth next to her. "Man, can you believe we won Songwriter of the Year? *Always* wanted to win that one."

Emma drew back, watching him. She crossed one hand over the other, resting them on the table. *This is a new life,* she told herself. *Stay calm.* She rolled on, despite hearing a part of her inner self laugh hysterically. "It's incredible. Awesome. But how did it happen exactly?" She pressed down hard on her hand, to keep both from trembling. Didn't work.

Jason stopped midway through a second whoop. "What?" He appeared perplexed for a second before his face relaxed. "Oh, you think I was saying it was just me? Hell, no. It was all your words. 'Wishsome.' So catchy. Man, isn't everybody here wishin' they'd written something like that." He chortled. "They're wishin' some, that's for sure."

A waitress appeared before them, wearing a smile so big it took over her face. "Welcome!" she bubbled.

"Hey, darlin'," drawled Jason, his accent taking on a life of its own. "Now aren't we lucky to have you waitin' on us this special evening?" He tipped his head and cocked his brows meaningfully at the trophy in the center of the table.

I just threw up a little, thought Emma.

"May I say congratulations, sir," said the waitress, her smile, impossible though it seemed, growing even bigger. She tore her gaze from Jason to include Emma. "To both of you."

"Why, thank you," Jason said. "It's a purty special night."

He did not just say *purty,* Emma thought. But he had. She pulled her mouth tight before giving the waitress an answering smile. Then she put her head in her hands, hoping the fingernails would quit scratching on the chalkboard.

"Can I bring you drinks?"

Emma wriggled her fingers toward her two glasses of champagne. She had yet to take a drink from either.

When she raised her head again, the waitress had left.

"Good to see you back," Jason said, back to his normal speaking voice. "Is somethin' wrong? Why aren't you jumping up and down? This is what we wanted. And it makes up for me not winning New Artist of the Year." He paused. "Well, almost does, anyway." He shook his head. "Damn, should have won Single of the Year, too, the way 'Wishsome' has been burnin' up the charts."

Emma nodded, as though she understood every bit of that.

"Wait a minute. You mad about the melody stuff? That's just between you and me, right?"

"Not mad." Emma kept nodding.

"Good." He thrummed his fingers on the table.

"But what about Chase Chapman?"

Jason's expression darkened. "I can't believe you're bringing up that guy. After what he did to you?" He shook his head. "Thank God he had the sense to leave town. Chapman didn't have a damn thing to do with that song and ain't nobody gonna say otherwise."

Chase had left town. Something had happened between them. While Emma processed this information, the waitress again appeared to slide two drinks before them. Apparently Jason had ordered for Emma.

She studied the pink concoction with an orange slice perched on the rim of the glass. Maybe it would help her navigate her new life, which had become damn confusing, all things considering. She took a tentative sip and coughed. Had to be ten percent pink and ninety percent alcohol.

Jason, on the other hand, had a glass of amber liquid on the rocks. He took a long swig and made a pleased sound. "Aw, man, good stuff." He leaned back against the leather. "What a night."

At last, something she could agree with. "What a night." Emma braved another sip of the drink, a bigger one this time, and watched the light play on the impressive crystal trophy. This time, she didn't cough from the alcohol content. Another sip seemed in order, so she took it, pushing aside the glasses of champagne.

"Here's to us." Jason raised his glass and waited for her to meet it. She picked up her glass and clinked it with his, then took another drink, the pink confection slipping down her throat more easily this time. Her new world was beginning to blur around the edges, which, at this point, suited her just fine.

She studied the man sitting next to her. Carefully cultivated stubble of dark whiskers and brown hair tousled to perfection with the requisite dent from the cowboy hat. Brown eyes framed by thick lashes, a long, straight nose—not too big and not too small—and white, even teeth. Not a feature out of place.

Jason Jeffries was handsome. In an assembly line kind of way. If you looked at him in a 360-degree view online, legs spread and arms out to his sides, you wouldn't find one thing out of place.

"Likin' what you see?" he asked with a wink. "Want a photo with your favorite guy?"

Caught. She felt the heat creep into her cheeks. "Uh, no. I—" Too late. He'd already whipped out an iPhone and was leaning toward her for the shot. *Flash.*

"I'll text it to you. Right after I tweet it."

He did, without even looking at it. She heard a ping from the purse beside her. Now *that* would be a good photo. Jason grinning and Emma looking like she'd been struck by lightning. Or a Madame Claire special.

Another drink of the pink stuff, which was seriously beginning to grow on her. She wondered if there was some sort of factory for rising country stars. *Now we need a blond one with a black hat!* she imagined a pudgy executive calling out. She giggled.

"I know. This is great, right?" Jason said with a wide grin.

Emma glanced out at the partiers, hoping to see food close by. "I need something to eat." Otherwise, her veins would shortly be flowing with pink alcohol.

"Don't worry about it, babe." Jason waved a hand. "I'll grab us something."

Before she could respond, he stepped out of the booth. Emma took another sip, letting the liquid roll around on her tongue. This might be her new favorite drink. Ever. A few minutes later, Jason was back with a plate piled so high with food, it tipped dangerously to one side.

"How did you know what I'd want?" She frowned. This was serious business. She was allergic to mushrooms.

A short laugh. "Ha, that's a good one. Like I don't know everything about you."

Her frown deepened, which wasn't easy as part of her face was beginning to numb. She hoped Jason Jeffries didn't know everything about her. There were parts of her she didn't like that much.

"Don't worry," he said. "No mushrooms in any of it. And no coconut, either. You hate that."

Oh crap. He did know her. So much for being mysterious.

He slid in beside her and leaned close to whisper in her ear, "You know, I was thinkin' I'd propose on the stage tonight when we won. Drop to one knee and everything. On camera."

Emma's jaw dropped. Jason drew back to give her a nod and a conspiratorial grin. "Wouldn't that have been great?"

"Great," she repeated. She did not even know this guy.

"Would have done it, too, if Etta Dorcas hadn't hustled you offstage so fast. Man, that sucks. The shot would have been in every magazine."

Her wedding proposal. In every magazine.

All she could think of, through the layer of fluffy pink cotton in her brain, was…*if I marry him, would he expect his jeans ironed every morning?*

CHAPTER FOUR

Jason Jeffries seemed determined to defeat the purpose of a quiet booth. The guy kept popping out to yell hello or to see if anyone he knew, or wanted to know, was close by. Emma knew she should be enjoying every second of this exclusive party, but she couldn't think straight with Jason on the move so much.

"Sit down," she hissed, though her hissing had been compromised by the second pink drink that had been put in front of her. She didn't remember ordering it, probably because she hadn't. But she downed it, anyway, stuffing pieces of warm bread in her mouth afterward in an attempt to soak up the alcohol.

She wished Chase were here to celebrate "Wishsome's" win. She wished Jason would go away. She wished...she could figure out why her life had been turned upside down in the space of a couple of hours.

"So, *Jason*," she began.

"Y-e-s, my very own pretty woman?" He winked at her.

She hesitated, not sure if that was a reference to the Roy Orbison song or the Julia Roberts movie. Didn't matter. Could be construed as a compliment either way. As long as he meant Julia Roberts at the *end* of the movie.

"You're wanting to know when the proposal is coming?" he went on. "I was just thinking about that and—"

"No!" Emma broke in. At Jason's startled look, she backpedaled. "I mean, of course, what girl wouldn't want to know, but we don't have to rush into anything, right?"

He blew out a *ha* sound as his fingers cradled his drink. "Oh yes, we do."

Oh God no. She wasn't preg—No, no, no.

Jason covered her hand with his and gave it a squeeze. "If we're gonna time our wedding with the album's release date, I'd best get to officially proposing. I mean we have the ring and everything. Nothing's stoppin' us."

Relief shot through her. "Right. The album. No other reason."

"What else is there?" He looked perplexed. "You're the one who keeps saying you need a proposal picture because it's so hard to come up with things to tweet."

Great. She'd turned into a person who would get married for Twitter material. "But we could delay the album release date, couldn't we? If we needed to."

Alarm spread across Jason's face. "Hell, no. Not unless we want to blow a hole through my career *and* yours."

"Oh. Right." Her nod was earnest, as though she knew exactly what he was talking about.

He cocked one eyebrow. "Speaking of the album, when are you going to get me lyrics for those three songs we still need?"

"Three?" Emma squeaked. She hadn't written lyrics to one song, let alone three, in, well, years.

"What is *wrong* with you tonight?" Jason puzzled. "You feeling all right?"

She was saved from having to answer by the appearance of the waitress, who carried more drinks. Pink liquid had never looked so good. Some spilled over the side as she lifted the glass to her lips.

"Hey, slow down," murmured Jason in an aside, even as he bestowed a dazzling smile on their waitress. "Don't want to get stuff all over that beautiful dress."

Emma looked down at the one-shouldered turquoise silk dress Taryn had helped her change into before leaving the awards venue. It *was* beautiful. In fact, she'd had a hard time believing it was her reflection in the mirror. Slimmer, with her dark blonde hair softly curling around her shoulders in an expensively casual way, her blue eyes brightened by what had to be a professional makeup job, and long earrings sparkling against her glowing skin.

Jason was right. She should be more careful. She rearranged the napkin in her lap, making each corner perfect, and straightened. Maybe all she had to do was act like the person she'd seen reflected in her mirror. Successful, confident. An *award* winner. Instead of being scared to death someone would come running up to point at her and yell, "Fake!"

She cleared her throat. "Tell me again about those songs. About your album."

His face lit up and he started talking. And talking. Emma knew she should be paying close attention, since she apparently might have to write some lyrics, but the candlelight, alcohol, and sparkling trophy conspired to send her into a kind of a dreamy haze, pierced only by the occasional words from Jason. Home, he said. Making it big. Bigger than love.

She paused, mid-sip on that one. What was bigger than love? But the question required too much thought. She lowered the glass and smiled sweetly at him, letting his husky voice take her back to that place where she didn't have to think. Didn't have to wonder when she would return to her real life. If it would happen when she was drunk enough to withstand the trip. Or when she was asleep. Or in the shower. *That* would suck.

Her drink kept getting refilled. She really had to find out what it was called, because she liked it. A lot.

Jason Jeffries was good looking. Really good looking, in that way you know there might not be a lot beneath the brim of the hat, but maybe you didn't care. She wondered if he'd been his high school's quarterback. If he'd had all the girls after him in that small town where he must have grown up, smelling like hay, summer nights and his father's after-shave. If he had a picture of himself at the age of two, in a too-big cowboy hat and matching boots.

Her head jerked abruptly and she realized she'd been propping it up with an elbow that had stopped cooperating.

He quit talking and reached out to move her drink a few inches away.

"No," she protested thickly. "I'm fine." She wasn't sure, but thought it came out sounding like the "f" had taken on a life of its own.

"You're not," she heard him say from somewhere above her. She closed her eyes. She felt a little dizzy, but that must have to do with the trip she'd taken today. All the way from an unemployed music teacher to a CMA winner.

Because of Chase. Where was he, anyway? How does a person fix her biggest regret when the subject of that regret didn't bother to show up for the fixing? A hiccup rocked her body and she clapped a hand to her mouth. "Sorry," she mouthed to someone's shirt.

Oh. Jason's shirt. They were on the move. Mostly him moving and her holding on.

"Congratulations!" she heard someone yell. As Jason lifted his hand, Emma felt herself slip down his body, catching her chin on his belt. "Ow," she said, rubbing skin in the general area of her chin. Her hand didn't seem to be receiving the right signals from her brain.

"Hold on there," Jason said, hoisting her back up. "Car's right outside."

"Where are we going?" she tried to ask, but it all seemed to come out in one word, which explained why there wasn't an answer.

A few minutes later, she sank onto the seat of a limo and toppled over onto her side. She heard a soft masculine chuckle somewhere above her and opened her eyes long enough to see Jason slide in beside her. She closed her eyes again.

The butter-soft leather against her cheek smelled of money. The kind of money that didn't have to be stretched until it turned inside out. The kind you didn't even have to think about; it was just there. As much as you needed.

She breathed in deep. And let the dark envelop her.

***

Emma woke with a start, sitting straight up in a strange bed with a sheet gripped in her fist. Her lips moved, but nothing came out except the half-strangled noises only a furry tongue and parched mouth could make.

Her temples pounded. Her hair stuck to her damp face and neck. Her stomach rolled over once, then twice.

She had no idea where she was. In front of her, tall curtains framed blinds that had sunlight peeking around the edges. The bed she was in was expansive, with a stark white duvet and sheets against dark wooden posts. A huge flat screen took over one wall.

Not good. A girl never wanted to wake up not knowing where she was, what she'd done, what she was…or wasn't…wearing. She mustered her courage to peer beneath the covers.

A shiny ivory bra, trimmed with the most delicate of lace, and its matching thong, directed accusations at her. So, she was in a strange house. Lying in a strange bed. Wearing strange beautiful underwear she couldn't possibly afford.

A door opened to her right and in walked Jason Jeffries, his hair rumpled and dark sweatpants riding low on his hips. His chest was bare and hairless, his nipples pale, his physique lean. A lot like a Ken doll. She wondered whether his chest could possibly be made of hard plastic.

Jason rounded the bed with ease and hopped onto the other side, causing the mattress to jump. Emma gripped the sheet even harder.

"You're awake," he said.

"Um, well. Yes." Her breathing was too fast.

"How do you feel?" A lazy grin stretched across his face.

"Not so good." *And the winner for Understatement of the Year…Miss Emma Zane!*

"Want some coffee?"

Her stomach turned over in response. She shook her head. Carefully.

"Okay. Want something else?" His fingers did a slow creep toward her across the massive bed.

Oh. She got it, now. That grin was meant to be a seductive one. *Crap*. She did not go to all the trouble to arrange this do-over—Wait. She hadn't exactly arranged this—*never mind*. She was here now and the last thing she wanted to do was sleep with someone she didn't even know, some guy whose idea of seduction was a wink and a game of itsy-bitsy-spider.

"What happened last night?" she demanded.

Jason started. His fingers halted, an inch from her leg. "I brought you back here."

"And did what?" She needed to brush her teeth. *Really* needed to.

He tipped his head, narrowing his eyes. "Nothing. I put you to bed so you could sleep it off. What are you trying to say?" He sounded offended. "You think I would have sex with you while you were passed out?"

"*Did* you?" Now she sounded petulant. But the fact that she couldn't remember what had happened after she entered the limo was circling her brain, causing a general panic amongst the cells that had survived the night.

"Emma." He withdrew his hand and rolled onto his back, staring up at the ceiling. "Are you kiddin' me? You think I'm that kinda guy? *Shit*."

He appeared genuinely offended. Remorse washed over her. She loosened her hold on the sheet, though she kept it over her. "It's just that—" She clamped her mouth shut.

He turned to her. "That what?"

She lifted a shoulder. "Sorry," she offered.

Jason heaved a sigh.

Emma felt even worse for about two seconds, before Jason suddenly brightened. "So, how about you get dressed and start writing those songs." He patted her sheet-covered leg. "I'll get you some aspirin and some breakfast. You write better on a full stomach."

Better than what? Jason had rounded the bed again, heading toward the door, before Emma found her voice. "I'm not writing a song right now." Getting dressed, finding out where she was, how she got here, where Chase had gone…those were *just a little* more important.

"Oh now, honey." Jason slid across the hardwood floor to her side. "I know you're not feelin' your best, but all you have to do is focus. Focus on writing the lyrics to three songs."

"I don't even know where to find my—"

"Writing pad?" That fast, he'd found one and put it in front of her.

She shook her head, desperate to make him understand. "No, my—"

"Pencil." He sat beside her and rummaged in the drawer of a nightstand, waving a freshly sharpened number two pencil in front of her.

"No!"

This time, Jason's sigh was less patient. "Emma. We need three songs. You can't keep putting that off." He raised his palms, imploring the ceiling. "What's going on?"

Emma hesitated. "Maybe I've lost, you know, my touch?" she suggested.

His laugh sounded more like an unhappy bark. "Those are words I never thought I'd hear from Emma Zane. Lost it. Right." He stood. "Are you kidding? You won Songwriter of the Year last night. You haven't lost *anything*. You're just getting started, woman."

Okay. One, she really hated being called "woman." Two, Jason Jeffries had a very unattractive vein standing out in his neck. Three, he wasn't acting like a man who was talking to his cherished unofficial fiancée. Four, oh hell. She didn't know what four was. She bent her head. "I don't know where to find my clothes."

"Your what?"

"*Clothes*." This time, she practically yelled it at him.

His expression softened into something that looked like tenderness.

Seriously, did the guy's emotions run at surface level *all* of the time?

"Why didn't you say so?"

"I tried."

He chucked her under the chin, much like he might do to the five-year-old child she felt like right now. "My cleaning lady already picked them up. You've got other clothes here. I moved them to the side in my closet." He gestured toward sliding doors that went all the way to the ceiling, "but they're still there."

His closet. Emma glanced at it and back at him. One piece of information secured. She was at Jason's house. In his bed, in her underwear. Feeling as though she'd just gone through the spin cycle in an unbalanced washing machine.

"So." He pointed toward the door. "I'm gonna get breakfast. You're gonna get dressed. And *we* are gonna get us some songs written."

Emma blinked.

Jason flashed her a smile. "That's my girl." Cheerful again, he left, closing the door behind him. She heard boots clattering on stairs, loud at first and then fading away.

Emma fixated on the bedroom window, wondering how many sheets she'd have to tie together to make an escape rope. And how long it would take Jason to notice she'd gone.

CHAPTER FIVE

Emma didn't use the rope she'd made by tying knots until her hands ached. She thought about it, opening the window to evaluate the drop and potential for bone breakage. But in the end, she wasn't the kind of a person who crawled out a window. She was a face-the-facts kind of a person. A very annoying trait at times.

So instead, she left the bedding, knots and all, in a pile on the floor and opened the closet that smelled of wood and leather to find women's clothing hanging in one corner, next to a small dresser. She opened one of the drawers to see Jason's underwear in it, arranged with precision and folded with knifelike edges. The next drawer she opened held what appeared to be a few changes of underwear for her.

After changing, she pulled on a soft, flowy shirt and a pair of skinny jeans. Then she rummaged through the drawer until she located socks to put on. She zipped up a pair of expensive-looking boots over them.

A hairbrush and brand-new toothbrush awaited her in the adjoining bathroom. Once she'd finished, she stopped before the mirror, taking in the result. Not bad. She had good taste in clothes when she had money.

Emma glanced toward the door. Time to face the music. Literally.

She found Jason sitting on a stool in an expansive kitchen downstairs, staring into a cup of coffee. He looked up with a smile and gave a low whistle. "You look nice."

"Thank you," she said, a little shyly. Maybe she could make it work with Jason, who seemed like a decent enough guy, even if he probably got manicures. And facials. No guy had skin that nice without help.

"Breakfast?" Jason pulled a pan and a stainless steel bowl from a cupboard and set them on the countertop. "My special egg-white omelet and mango smoothie, coming right up."

"Thank you."

Chase had once made her cinnamon toast at his house, heavy on the sugar, light on the cinnamon. Just the way she liked it. He'd accidentally burned it around the edges, which gave it a satisfying crunchiness. Once he'd gone, she'd never been able to make cinnamon toast without thinking about him.

Jason tied an apron around his waist. An apron. Without a single spot on it. Did the man never spill anything? He'd be in for a rude awakening with Emma here, queen of spill-it, sponge-it, forget-it.

Emma straightened her shoulders and climbed carefully onto the stool Jason had vacated. She folded her hands in front of her, feeling as though this breakfast offering required a certain degree of formality. "You're a chef?" She meant it as a statement, but it came out as a question.

"This country boy? Only in my dreams." He winked at her.

Holy hell. Another wink. She shuddered before she could stop herself and then blurted her next words to cover for the shuddering. "I need to find Chase."

Jason's expression hardened and he stopped mid-egg separation. "Why? What does he have to do with anything?" His country accent had faded.

Emma focused on a yellow yolk that looked poised to sneak its way out of the shell and into the bowl of egg whites. "It's nothing to do with—" she pointed at Jason and then herself "—the two of us. It's just that…There's something I need to talk with him about." She suspected she did, anyway. "More of an unfinished business thing." Her voice trailed away, squirming under Jason's narrow-eyed gaze.

"Unfinished business," he repeated.

She nodded and then pointed. "That yolk is going to—"

"With a guy who left you because you sold me lyrics to make rent."

She ducked her head to give herself a chance to process what he'd said. She'd sold lyrics to Jason? That's why Chase had left? Something wasn't making sense here. A whole lot of something.

From the corner of her eye, she saw Jason drop the rest of the egg in the bowl, yolk and all, to lean closer to her. "You're not acting like the Emma Zane I know." A brief hesitation. "And love, by the way."

By the way? She didn't want to be loved by the way. She wanted to be loved wholly, genuinely, passionately. Like Chase had loved her.

Once upon a time.

She lifted her chin to meet Jason's eyes.

"You said you were through with him. Never wanted to see him again." Jason's voice rose on the last word. She thought she heard a note of desperation in it.

He averted his gaze, splaying his fingers on the granite countertop and pushing hard until the tips turned white. He wasn't as sure of himself as she'd thought. There might…just might…be a crack in the Ken doll's plastic.

Emma sucked in a breath and said, "He co-wrote 'Wishsome.'"

Jason's upper lip disappeared. "The *hell* he did."

"He helped me write the lyrics."

"*No* one helps you write lyrics. You won't even let me be in the same room until you're done with them. I figured we'd have to use two rooms today."

Really? She'd always written lyrics with Chase in the room, strumming on his guitar. They'd tried out bits and pieces to see what would work and what wouldn't. This didn't make sense. "Well, he did," she said softly.

Jason heard it. "What's going on, Emma?" he said, his voice tight. "First, you're acting all polite, as if you don't even know me, and then you start talking about Chase Chapman. Saying you want to see him, when I know for a fact he is the last person you want to see. And he's the last person *I* want you to see." He stopped for a breath and stood to face her, hands jammed onto his hips. "Doesn't that count for anything?"

Words leapt to her lips. *I'm sorry. I don't know what's going on. Sure, what you say should count for something.* But they melted on her tongue before they could make it out of her mouth. Instead, she lifted one shoulder and relied on her eyes to relay her confusion.

Jason apparently wasn't fluent in reading eyes. He shook his head. "And now you're being coy."

Did a country boy ever use the word "coy"? She didn't think so. She was beginning to suspect his roots were more Chicago than Chattanooga, as he'd claimed in the magazine article she'd read.

"Like I'm some kind of a toy," he finished, sounding injured. Then he stopped, his brows narrowing in surprise.

"You rhymed," Emma suggested.

"I did." He crossed the room to a kitchen cupboard, pulling out a pad of paper and pen. "Better write that down."

If he had to write that down, he didn't write lyrics very often. She sighed, wondering if she was contracted for those three songs and whether they had to be good. Because she wasn't sure she was any good any more. If she ever had been.

"Wishsome" had to have been a fluke. The last good song she'd ever write. At least she had an award to commemorate her one-hit wonder-ness.

"I'd better go."

Jason looked up. He put the pen down and turned, clasping his hands in front of him. "Emma."

She stood, pushing the stool back with her legs. "No, really. I have to go." She put her palms out in front of her, warning him away.

"I'm sorry. I didn't mean to upset you. I know you don't like it when someone questions you."

Only the handful of students who regarded music class as a joke. "It's not that."

"Then tell me what it is. Let me make it right." He crossed the room to enfold her in a hug, smashing her warning palms against her chest. "Let's plan the proposal right now, somethin' big, somethin' that'll be splashed all over the magazines."

His accent was back, she noted, also taking in that he smelled like lemon soap and dry-cleaning.

"We can do it before the record releases," he continued. "Sure, we can. Maybe we'll get *married* on release day. Yeah, that's it. A great idea."

He sounded enormously pleased with himself for thinking of such a good solution. Emma, on the other hand, wanted to throw up. She recovered use of her hands enough to push him away. Hard.

"Emma. Baby."

She, who was fluent in eyes, could see his injured look. She just couldn't tell how authentic it was. And, really? Baby?

On the same built-in kitchen desk where Jason had been writing, she spotted a Gucci purse. Had to be hers. There weren't any other women here. At least not any she'd noticed. And if she'd ever had enough money, she would have purchased that exact purse. A little part of her heart, the part that often longed for things she'd never had, lifted.

She skirted around Jason to the desk and picked up the purse, clutching it hard. "Thank you for offering to make breakfast. That's so nice of you. And I'm sure it would be delicious, but I really have to leave."

"How?"

Already heading in the direction of where the front door must be, she stopped mid-step. "What?"

"How are you going to leave? Your car isn't here."

"I'll call a cab." She hoped she'd find a cell phone and some money in that purse. And a driver's license would be helpful, since she didn't exactly know where home was.

He sighed. "I'll drive you." He scooped up a pair of keys. "At least let me do that much."

All but the practical side of her, which was accustomed to winning any internal argument, shouted *no way*. "Okay," she said. "Thank you."

Jason shot her a strange look before shoving a cowboy hat on his head. "You're awful polite this morning." He put a hand on the small of her back, steering her out of the front of the house and to a waiting pickup truck that gleamed in the morning sunlight. "Your chariot, ma'am." He opened the door for her.

Minutes later, he pulled the truck to a stop in front of a dark brown, cottage-style house with a white picket fence edged in bright purple flowers. "That house is adorable," Emma breathed.

"It should be," Jason said, sounding perplexed. "You've put enough into renovating it."

Emma loved the steep pitched entry, bright white trim, and the red brick walkway. There was something cozy and the tiniest bit fairy-tale about the house. She would not have been the least bit surprised to see Glinda step out the front door in full Good Witch of the North regalia, bearing a plate of cookies.

Jason opened the truck door for her to step out and followed her gaze. "At least you'll get your money out of it when you sell."

This was the first time she'd owned a house. "Why would I ever sell it?"

"Call me old-fashioned, but I'd like my wife livin' with me."

Oh. That again. "Right," she said, meaning *wrong*. She'd deal with that later.

Right now, she had a house—her first-ever, very own house—to explore. Not to mention a first love to find.

CHAPTER SIX

The house turned out to be as amazing on the inside as it had promised to be from the outside. It had taken some doing to get Jason to leave, though. In the end, she'd had to swear to him she would work on the songs she owed. Then she'd practically pushed him out the door before shutting it firmly in his face.

Turned out the new Emma was more assertive than the old Emma. Not that she'd set that bar very high in her former life.

Now she was alone. In her own house. *Okay, Madame Claire, two points for you. And throw in an extra point for the Gucci purse.* This was the life she could have had if she'd gone to Nashville? Nice.

She removed her shoes and laid them carefully next to the door, afraid to track anything onto the pine floors.

The house was furnished mostly in white, with a mix of modern sofas and chairs and what appeared to be antique cabinets and tables. The moldings, fixtures and doors looked original to the early part of the twentieth century but had been carefully restored. In the kitchen, granite counters and stainless-steel appliances nested companionably against antique cabinets with leaded glass fronts.

Damn. If she'd been responsible for any part of this restoration, she'd handled it well. Every room she walked through, she said, "This is *mine.*" But no matter how many times she said it, she still couldn't believe it.

After checking out the master bedroom, she climbed a narrow set of stairs to find another bedroom, with an adjacent small library tucked beneath a sloping roof. A headboard of polished wood rose above cheerful blue and white bedding, and a vase on the nightstand held fresh peonies. Emma stopped for a long, soul-cleansing sniff and smiled before dropping into an overstuffed chair in the corner of the room.

She closed her eyes and laid her hands across her middle as she sank into the soft cushions. Growing up, she and her mother had lived in a series of places, each as colorless and devoid of personality as the next. As an adolescent, Emma had tried to brighten things up, but she gave up after a while. Why do anything? They were only going to move again. Soon.

Her mother had a bad habit of believing everything she heard. Even, or maybe especially, when those things came from men who, on the surface, seemed to have good intentions. Old photos showed that Trina Zane had once been slim and beautiful, with lively blue eyes, bouncy blonde hair and porcelain skin. But when she became pregnant with Emma at sixteen, she'd dropped out of high school, trusting her sixteen-year-old boyfriend when he'd sworn he'd take care of everything.

He had apparently tried, until his parents yanked him away, moving the whole family to another state before Emma was born. Trina had taken a minimum-wage job while her parents cared for her baby. That had ended when Trina's parents were killed in a car accident shortly after she turned 19.

She'd met another man who she said "didn't have an unkind bone in his body" and trusted him to invest the small inheritance she'd received. Unfortunately, he also didn't have a financial bone in his body, it seemed, as the money had all been gone within a year. "That's okay," Trina had told her young daughter in what became a familiar refrain over the years. "Everything will work out. You'll see."

Emma had seen, all right. After four broken engagements, one brief marriage, a stool she called her own at the local casino, and too many non-winning lottery tickets to count, Trina Zane's captivating looks had taken on a blurred weariness. Her blonde hair faded to a darker ash lined with gray and her eyes only sparkled when yet another man invited her back to the land of promises.

Emma moved out at eighteen and her relationship with her mother had become increasingly strained by the older woman's willingness to accept the latest line she'd been fed. It felt as though the parent/child roles had been reversed, as though Emma was the one who had to watch out for her mother, warn her away from potential harm, save her from perpetual naiveté. She hated it and felt the resentment build inside her like a tumor resistant to treatment. But she kept doing it.

Somebody had to. It was just the two of them, had always been just the two of them.

And then, Emma had lost her job and her mother had become the sole wage-earner, working as an assistant to the owner of a small accounting firm. Mr. Kramer was pudgy, bald and married. He loved to flirt, make inappropriate jokes and claim bonuses would be handed out all around soon. They weren't, probably because Mr. Kramer also loved to spend his company's money on lavish outings with potential clients who didn't sign on the dotted line. But according to Trina, he was kind and benevolent, only acting with the best of intentions.

Emma's stomach tightened, sensing another blade soon about to swipe at her mother's ready heart. Even worse, none of the "surgeons" worked with precision. They took their toll with a dull knife that sawed away until Trina was left spent and suffering.

Emma pushed her mother's problems from her mind, not to resurface for at least…another ten minutes.

She floated back to the realization that she was sitting in a house she owned. In a chair she owned. With her feet on a rug she owned.

For the first time ever, she had a place she could call "home." Hers, all hers.

Her eyes flew open. Maybe, in Emma's new life, her mother's life was comfortably stable and the worry that sat like a five-pound weight on Emma's shoulders didn't need to be there after all.

She reached into the Gucci handbag she'd set beside her, searching for a cell phone. A minute later, she had it in her hand and was calling the number stored as "Mom."

When she heard the voice mail message, Emma's heart lifted. Her mother sounded happier than Emma had heard her in years. "Hi, Mom," she said. "It's me. Just calling to see how you are. Call me back. Okay…" She gulped before finishing with, "Love you."

Emma clicked off the phone and laid her head against the back of the chair. Before he left, Jason had told her she wouldn't get paid until all songs for the new record were done. He'd made it sound like a reminder, as though he'd had to tell her that before. Hopefully, that wasn't because the award-winning songwriter she was today was just as scared and certain she wouldn't be able to produce as the music teacher she was yesterday.

What the hell had Madame Claire done?

Given her what she'd always wanted—a chance to believe in Chase. And look what she'd done with it.

She had to find him. She hadn't gone through all of this to be here, in this new life, without him. And if she'd wronged him, she had to make it right. But really? He'd left because she'd sold lyrics to Jason Jeffries? Hold on. *Why* had she sold lyrics to Jason Jeffries? He'd said it was because she had to make rent, which sounded like a pretty desperate situation. Or Jason wasn't telling the truth.

Mattel wouldn't like that. Very un-Ken-like behavior.

Emma gave a half-snort, half-cry. Longing rippled through her that momentarily stole her breath. She missed Chase so much, missed his arms around her, his husky voice in her ear, the way he looked at her, as if she was so much more than she'd ever thought she could be.

She missed the…just admit it, cliché or not…*magic* they'd made when a song came together. Her words, his melody. Two halves that made a whole. Madame Claire had been right; the regret of not going with him to Nashville had burned a pinhole in her heart, leaving her unable to function at full capacity, always held back by what could have been.

And the promise of seeing him again, of getting another chance with him, had blown a cannonball straight through the pinhole.

Enough. She loved the house, loved the CMA award that now sat gleaming on her table, winking at her in the sunlight streaming through the window. Loved the fact she had a Gucci purse and an assistant.

At the same time, she hated that Chase wasn't here to enjoy it with her. What if this do-over had an expiration date? A chime on the hour could turn this house back into a cramped apartment and the Lexus she'd seen outside back to being a Toyota Corolla.

Emma rose from the chair and went to the window. With fingers curled around the edge of the curtain, she gazed outside at the peaceful neighborhood. She could only think of one way to track Chase down and that was to call his parents.

She didn't know the Chapmans well, but had had dinner with them a few times while she and Chase were together. Her memory of them was fuzzy, but the impression they'd left was of quiet, affable, sturdy parents who hovered in the background, watching over their brood. They had seemed baffled by Chase's musical ambitions but supported him nonetheless. The sort of *Growing Pains* environment Emma had longed for as a child, where life with the Seaver family was securely rooted in love and laughter in all the right places.

Half an hour and two wrong Chapman families later, Emma found Chase's father.

"Yes," he acknowledged stiffly, in contrast to the warm hello he'd answered with. "I remember you."

Emma pushed on. "I was hoping you could help me locate Chase. I don't have a current phone number or address for him." She'd gone through all of the contacts on her phone. Nothing.

Silence on the other end of the phone. Then, "Why do you need to contact my son?"

My son. If what Jason had said was true, she probably couldn't blame Mr. Chapman for his protectiveness. "There was a misunderstanding. A big one. I need to set things straight."

He was silent so long, she wasn't sure he was still on the line. Then he said, "Some misunderstandings are better left alone."

"*Are* they?" The words flew out of her mouth before she could stop them, her voice arching with dismissiveness. "I didn't mean that," she hastened to say, though she was pretty sure she had. If this was the way she spoke to people now, she didn't like it any more than they did. "There's some money owed to him." How the hell had "Wishsome" become a hit song without him?

"Money." The statement was flat, disbelieving.

"And an explanation."

"I will give you his email address. You can send him both."

No email, no PayPal. Wasn't going to happen. Emma had to see him.

"The thing is—" What exactly *was* the thing? "It has to go by mail. He has to sign for it," she lied. Since when did lies come so smoothly to her, zipping out of her mouth with zero-to-ninety acceleration?

He went silent again, apparently mulling his options. "Fine," he said at last. "I will give you his address." Emma heard some fumbling with paper and then Mr. Chapman said, "Post Office Box—"

"No!" she interrupted. "It can't...I mean there has to be a street address for the letter to be delivered." She crossed her fingers behind her back, hoping that would somehow make the fib less deceitful.

"For Post Office purposes only. I don't want you thinking you're going there. To see him."

He sounded a lot like the dad on *Growing Pains,* which made Emma's answer catch in her throat before she could manage to say, "Of course not."

A sigh, a hesitation and then he gave her a street address, concluding with, "Maven, Ohio."

Her pen stopped, hovering above the scrap of paper she'd found. "Ohio?"

"Southern Ohio. Down close to Kentucky. Not that it matters to the Post Office. I hear they'll deliver just about anywhere." His voice held a note of fatherly steel.

In that moment, she knew for certain that Jason had given her a very one-sided version of what had happened with Chase. Emma had to have been terrible to Chase, and given the way she apparently treated people now, she could believe it.

Somehow, it was worse to find out for yourself that you were less than a nice person than to have someone else point it out.

"Yes, they do," she agreed, silent apologies layered into the words. "So that should take care of things." *I'd do anything not to hurt him. Please believe me.*

"All right, then."

An awkward pause. "Thank you, Mr. Chapman. I appreciate it."

"Yes," he said. "Goodbye." A sharp click in her ear and he was gone.

Emma, on the other hand, was just getting started.

CHAPTER SEVEN

One of the keys she found in her purse turned smoothly in the ignition of the Lexus and the car jumped to life. Emma entered the address Chase's father had given her into the navigation system. Seven hours, fifty-one minutes.

Could be worse things than a road trip in this car, with its leather seats and state-of-the-art sound system, ready to do her bidding. As a satellite country music station played, she backed the car out of the driveway, creeping along, afraid of even the possibility of a scratch.

She and the Lexus, which she really hoped was hers, glided together through the streets together and onto the freeway. On the seat next to her rested a practical black suitcase, stuffed with clothes she'd found in the closet. It had taken her less time to decide to go see Chase and pack her clothes than it usually took her to decide if she would deviate, for a change, from her standard Starbucks order. She always ended up ordering the same coffee drink, but she thought about going with something different. A lot.

The sky was bright, even through her sunglasses, and the other drivers inexplicably polite. She followed the directions of the GPS, which, according to the signs, was steering her toward Louisville. Nice. She'd never been to Louisville.

For a while, she hung out behind a semi-truck from the Bob Evans restaurants, oddly comforted by the cheerful red and yellow sign and the picture of a white farmhouse. People there probably greeted you with a "*howdy*," she thought. Maybe she'd look for one when she got hungry.

The truck pulled off at an exit. She gave the driver a wave as she passed him, hoping it would release some of the nervous energy that was making her heart pound and occasionally skip a beat. Chase. She was going to see Chase. Would he push her out the door, the way she had Jason, before she even had a chance to explain she wasn't herself? She couldn't tell him why. Madame Claire's words were burned into her brain. Tell anyone and *all will unravel most unpredictably.*

Just what she needed. More unpredictability.

The miles rolled on. She looked for a new freeway friend to follow before vaguely realizing she was singing along to the song on the radio. Weird. The words tumbled out with gusto, with confidence. As though she knew this song. Which she did not. She'd never heard it before.

The part of her brain that was singing along to the words didn't respond to the part of the brain that told her it couldn't do that. Emma just kept on singing.

She pushed the info button to see that it was a song by Jason Jeffries. Emma had probably written it. The highway bobbed and weaved before her eyes and she found herself wishing for her Bob Evans truck friend. Some semblance of normality to hang on to.

The song's melody was country-pop, not great, but catchy. The words, though…they were pretty damn good.

Emma rubbed her forehead. She didn't like this. Didn't like it at all. The only thing worse than worrying whether you were good enough to do something was the knowledge that you once had been.

That CMA trophy would likely be the last one she'd ever win. She'd better keep it clean and polished.

The song stopped abruptly, replaced by the ring of a phone and the display of the word "Mom" on the screen.

Emma's heart did its familiar sink before she clenched her stomach muscles tight and steeled herself.

After fumbling with the buttons for a minute, she located the right one. "Mom?"

"Emmy!"

"How are you?"

"Good!"

She sounded like she meant it. Emma's hopes slid from the cage she kept them in to slither upward. "Great. What's going on?"

"Oh honey, the realtor called and I went to see the house you're buying me. I still can't believe you'd do that."

That makes two of us. I'm buying my mom a house?

"It's beautiful, just beautiful." A girlish giggle. "My friends will be so jealous. Who would have thought I'd ever live anyplace so nice? I feel like I should be going in the back entrance, not the front door."

"I'm glad you like it, Mom." Emma allowed a little of her breath to escape. She'd always wanted to be in a position to help her mother's life stabilize. And never imagined she would be.

"Are you sure you can afford it?"

Not at all. "Of course I can. Don't worry about that." *I'll do enough worrying for both of us. Always have.* Emma adjusted the visor to match the changing position of the sun.

"Well, thank you again, honey. Thank you so much."

"I'm your daughter. That's the way it should be." She would do anything for her mother. Emma had just begun feeling bad about remembering that she'd wanted to be a part of the family on *Growing Pains* when she heard her mother's breezy voice again.

"*Any*hoo," Trina's voice went up a few octaves. "Guess what?"

In Emma's experience, the words "Guess what" were never a prelude to something good. It was her mother's way of introducing something she knew Emma wouldn't like. *Guess what? The grocery store had a sale on liver and that's what we're having for dinner. Guess what? We're moving to a new place tomorrow and it doesn't have a laundry room, but it's cheaper than this place! Guess what…I'm getting married again and this time, it's going to work. He's different.*

Emma thought about breaking the connection and claiming it was the cell service. But in the end, she said, "What."

"I quit my job! Just like you said I should."

"I did? You did?"

"But my boss, Mr. Kramer—I mean, Bill. He said I should call him Bill, now. He was so sad. He said he's hoping we can still be friends. He wants to take me to the casino tonight; he knows how much I love going."

"Friends."

Her mother's voice wavered for a second and then plunged ahead. "He just separated from his wife. I think he's lonely. And he's such a nice man—"

"Don't do it," Emma broke in.

"Oh, Emmy, it's not a date or anything."

"What if his wife finds out and *she* thinks it's a date?"

A sigh. "I can't say no. I don't want to hurt his feelings."

"Stop!" That surprising, sharp bite was back. This time, it wasn't a bad thing. Her mother quit talking, something she almost never did, because talking over Emma was a tried-and-true method of making sure she didn't have to hear what her daughter had to say.

Emma's voice thundered through the car until she was sure the friendly looking family in the next car, with their dog's head hanging out of the car window and their tent trailer rolling behind them, could hear. "Tell him he can call you when his divorce is final. *Maybe*."

"Oh." Silence. Then, "If you think that's best."

Seriously? Her mother had just listened to her. More importantly, she'd just detoured off the no-way-is-this-going-to-end-well highway.

Emma pressed her shoulder blades into the leather seat. "I do."

"Okay."

"Okay?" Emma had to check.

"Yes, I said so."

"Good. That's good, Mom. I'm proud of you."

"Well, thank you, Emmy."

"Go pick out some furniture for your new house," Emma said, feeling uproariously happy. She waved at the dog in the next car. He eyed her suspiciously and barked.

"You know, I've played 'Wishsome' so many times, I think I've scratched the CD," her mother said. "It's such a good song and that Jason seems so sweet."

Sweet was her mother's highest compliment. "Ummm, yes. Sweet."

"I will let you go, honey. I know you're busy, being such an important songwriter."

Oh, if she only knew. Emma was a fraud, posing as a songwriter. "Wait. Mom—"

Her mother spoke at the same time, so she didn't hear. "Bye." The phone disconnected.

The car of the dog and tent trailer toting family picked up speed and sailed past her. Emma watched the dog's pink tongue disappear as he pulled his head inside, likely to play with his kids, who had to be going on a fun camping adventure with their parents.

Emma had never been camping in her life. For a brief moment, she wondered what they'd do if she pulled alongside them at the next rest stop and asked if she could come. She'd be content to squeeze between the kids in the back seat and hold the dog on her lap, even if he was the drooling type. At the campsite, she'd chop firewood and make soup, or whatever food you made while camping, and yell at the bears to keep them away from her new family.

Anything they wanted.

If only they'd allow her to go camping with them. Disappear. Just for a little while.

***

It was evening before the navigation system announced she would arrive at her destination, which was on the left, in 400 feet.

Thank God. She'd endured more dark, winding country roads than she'd ever cared to make the acquaintance of. Was all of southern Ohio one big, rolling farm? It felt that way.

She'd had to switch to a news station on the satellite radio. "Wishsome" had played so many times on the country and pop stations, she now had the melody committed to heart, where she didn't want it to live. She and Chase had been working on a ballad, but the song had turned into country-pop crossover.

The worst thing was that she couldn't decide if she hated that. Or not.

A voice interrupted. The GPS, announcing she'd reached her destination. As if it were a normal place. As if she wasn't about to see the man she'd never forgotten, the man who had occupied a part of her heart for so long, she'd never been able to give it to anyone else.

Maybe that was all she needed or would get from this do-over. Closure.

She signaled left, not that there was another car anywhere to see, and turned.

Gravel crunched beneath her tires. Trees along the road obscured any sign of a house, so it was a relief when it came into view, looming large against the darkening sky. No lights on.

Oh. She hadn't thought about what to do if he wasn't home. Camp out on his front porch?

She stopped the car. The wooden porch was an expansive one, with a cushioned swing in the corner. Easy to imagine Chase with his guitar on a lazy day, wearing a crisp white t-shirt, one muscular leg resting on the wood, the other pushing the swing back and forth in a steady rhythm. His hands, tanned and strong, would be…

Enough. She was picturing Chase from several years ago. He wouldn't be the same now, just as she wasn't. *No,* whispered that annoying voice from inside her, *he'll look even better now.*

Emma had had more than enough of that voice. For all she knew, Chase had drunk himself into a stupor and had a puffy, lined face and a stomach that rolled over his belt, no matter how hard he tried to cinch it in.

Because he's brokenhearted? Think an awful lot of yourself, don't you?

"Oh, shut *up*," she said aloud. Even when she argued with herself, she couldn't win.

She hugged herself tight, watching the house and thinking. This hadn't been in the plan. Chase was supposed to be inside, next to a cozy, crackling fire. Waiting for her, though he didn't know it. When he saw her, his face would light up with equal parts of relief and happiness. That's when she would know it would all be okay, that they could work out whatever had happened. That Jason Jeffries couldn't have told her the whole truth.

So…on to Plan B. Whatever that was.

A sound not far from the car caught her attention. Wildlife scurrying by, off to her left. As of now, curling up on the porch swing to wait for Chase was out of the question. All she needed was to be awakened by the curious poke of a deer antler in her eye. She wondered if a deer mother ever told her son to be careful with those things or he'd put someone's eye out.

She chortled, more from nervous disappointment than thinking it was funny. *Damn.* She'd been so sure she could walk in and find him, set things straight, and live happily ever after with Chase. Why did nothing she made up in her head ever turn out the way she'd imagined?

Furious with herself, Emma swiped at a traitorous tear with the back of her hand and put the car in drive. As she turned to head back down the long driveway, something caught her eye. A light. Coming from a building to the left of the house and set back further from the road.

She peered closer. From the outline, it appeared to be a barn.

Her heart stopped mid-beat. *Chase.*

CHAPTER EIGHT

Chase thought he heard a noise from outside the barn. He paused in his hammering. There had been some kids trespassing on land lately, he'd heard in town. Teenagers. Mostly harmless, but probably up to no good.

He listened hard. Nothing. Either he was hearing things or it was some sort of visiting wildlife.

He positioned the nail and pounded it in place, angry at himself all over again that he had to build these cabinets from scratch. Nothing he'd worked on had survived his drunken rampage. The sharp, determined sound of hammering helped him a little, though. At least it was action.

Lila lifted her head and growled. Hell, something or someone *was* outside. The dog was never wrong.

Chase moved swiftly but silently to the door of the barn. He held up for a minute, listening, and then slid it open hard.

Someone stood there. Someone who took a sharp intake of breath in the stillness. He blinked, convinced he couldn't be seeing right. It looked like—Fuck, no. It couldn't be. Not—

She spoke. "Hello, Chase."

Emma.

Her eyes met his and for a moment, something inside him, maybe it was his heart, maybe it was something else, stutter-stepped. He wasn't sure he was breathing. If he was, it wasn't steady breathing. God, he'd missed her so much. Not only missed, but physically ached for her. And now she stood in front of him in a pool of light spilling from the barn, dressed in a white t-shirt that strained to confine her tits and cut off above her flat stomach, jeans that hugged her slim curves and long silver earrings. And on her feet, fuckin' take-me-now pointy heels. He could swear he saw her pulse jumping rapid fire in her neck.

His own pulse had probably imploded already.

"Emma." His voice caught. He saw her body relax, her knees sagging with what looked like relief.

His fingers tightened on the doorjamb. The memory of hearing "Wishsome," with that shit-ass melody from that shit-ass Jason

Jeffries, pierced his brain. And all of the warmth that had gone through him at the sight of Emma turned cold. Ice cold.

She didn't move. He didn't move.

A long moment passed, punctuated only by the growl of the dog at Chase's side, the rustle of a breeze through nearby trees, the soft tinkling of Emma's earrings, and the lonely call of an animal a distance away.

"What are you doing here?" he demanded, the question scraping against his suddenly raw throat.

She looked down at the ground, then back at him. "I don't know. I really don't."

"That's helpful." He hated the way he sounded, hated that she deserved nothing less.

"What are you doing in Ohio? Did you buy this place?"

"It was my grandfather's. He died. I'm helping my parents by fixing the place up." He took a deep breath, hoping it would calm him. "How did you find me?"

"Your dad gave me your address."

"He wouldn't do that."

"He did."

"What did you tell him?"

"That I needed to find you."

"Why?" Chase folded his arms across his chest. They stared at each other. Lila flopped at his feet with a grunt.

Emma jammed a hand on her hip, which was apparently a mistake because those stupid, dead-sexy shoes looked to be pretty hard to balance on in the dirt. She wobbled and then put her free hand on the side of barn. His mind registered that their fingers were less than a yard apart. Might as well have been miles.

"I was hoping we could talk."

"Talk." His eyes narrowed.

"We owe each other that much."

They owed each other a hell of a lot more than that. But he was pretty sure he'd never survive the payback.

"Sorry," she mumbled. "I never should have come." She turned too fast in the dirt and nearly fell. He reached out to catch her, but she waved him away, yanking off first one shoe and then the other to clutch them in her hand. They had red soles. And her naked toes were vulnerable, alluring, the nails also painted red. He'd always loved her toes and remembered that one, just one, was crooked. They'd laughed about it. In bed, the covers thrown to the floor.

"Just forget I was here, okay?" she said. She looked ready to bolt.

He wasn't going to let her. Stupidest thing he could do, but he wasn't going to let her leave. Not yet, anyway.

Chase looked down and gave a short, sharp whistle. "Lila, come." The dog leapt to her feet and followed him out of the barn doorway. Chase turned and slammed the door of the barn shut, plunging them all into darkness. "Follow me," he ordered Emma, and he took off down the path.

He could hear her padding along behind him with much smaller steps.

"Slow down," she called.

"Keep up."

"I would if I could."

He was being an ass. He knew it. And right now he didn't care.

She was still behind him when he stopped at the back of the house. He climbed a couple of steps and opened the door, flipping a switch that flooded the room with light. Then he went inside, going to the sink in the small kitchen, turning on the water and grabbing a bar of soap to wash the sawdust and dirt from his hands.

When Emma tried to put her foot inside, Lila plopped her butt on the linoleum floor, blocking her. Emma withdrew her foot and remained standing on the top step. "Excuse me?" she tried politely.

Lila held her position, denying Emma entry to the farmhouse.

"Um, if I could just get around you…" Emma lifted her foot to step to the right. The dog moved to the right. "Fine. I'll go this way, then." She tried scooting in to the left of Lila.

No such luck. That move was blocked, as well, with a low growl. Chase fought hard to hide his smile. Even harder to keep from saying, "Good dog."

Out of options, Emma looked around the doorjamb and up at Chase. "Maybe I should go to the front door."

"Won't help." He shut the water off, causing the pipes to clank, dried his hands with a towel and walked over to pull at the dog's collar. "Come on, Lila. You can take a chunk out of her later."

Lila hesitated but ultimately allowed Chase to lead her away.

Emma stepped inside.

"So," he said. "Have you decided yet why you're here? Or does Lila have to get it out of you?"

"You, uh, missed a spot." Emma pointed at his face, but her finger crumpled under his gaze. She put her hands behind her back.

Damn. He probably had dirt all over his face, which would screw with his plan to make her sorry she'd ever left him. That prick Jeffries probably showered four times a day. He picked up the towel again and swiped at his cheeks.

Lila growled.

"It's fine now," Emma said, shooting a sideways glance at Lila. "You got it."

Chase sent the towel sailing over to the counter. "This way." He led the way out of the kitchen and down a hallway into a large room with several scattered chairs, a large, scarred wooden table and two brown leather couches that had seen better days at least a decade ago. They had suited his grandfather fine. They suited Chase fine.

A mug sat on the coffee table, along with his Kindle, laptop and assorted chargers. Framed family pictures on the walls held stubbornly to layers of dust. Now that he saw the place through Emma's eyes, Chase realized how little he'd done so far to clean things up.

Emma peered closer at a picture of a very young Chase seated at an upright piano. His fingers hovered happily above the keys and he looked to be imploring the camera for permission to play.

"You?" Emma gestured toward the photograph.

"Not that it matters, but yes." He kept his voice cold.

Chase sank onto the nearest couch, his arms resting on the back and the arm. He put a boot on the coffee table. Lila jumped up to take a place beside him, laying her head on his leg. He wanted to invite Emma to sit down, but he couldn't afford to give even a hint of friendliness. It might lead to other things, things he couldn't control. "Congratulations on your award."

Emma lifted her chin. "You deserved one, too."

Surprise flickered through him. Of all the things he'd thought she might say, that wasn't one. He cleared his throat and thumped his fingers across the back of the sofa. "Bullshit. Wasn't my melody. I wouldn't have written that crap."

"I know." Emma eased herself into a chair opposite him. "You would have written it a lot better. You did. Started to, anyway."

Yeah, the one fucking song he'd never been able to finish. Great time to bring it up. He could sense a wood-splintering session coming on. "Didn't. Never finished it. But I guess you finally did. Or at least a version of it."

"Lucky me."

"I'd say so." His fingers tapped out an invisible beat against the sofa back.

"It should have been you and me up there."

He flinched. Once he'd found out Emma was nominated, he'd watched the CMAs on his grandfather's ancient TV that only got three channels and gave everything a pink tinge. Despite the bad reception, Emma had looked more beautiful than he'd ever seen her. Except for—Shit, *now*.

He'd also seen Jason Jeffries hanging all over her. And wanted to kill him for it.

This conversation right here, right now wasn't going to end up anywhere good. As his grandfather used to say, *too much water under the bridge.* In this case, the water was over his head. "No you and me about it," he said at last. "You had a choice to make and you made it. End of story."

Emma clenched her fist. "It was never like you thought."

"Really." The hand that he had petting Lila picked up speed. The dog looked up at him, questioning. "It wasn't that you went behind my back to find a new writing partner." *Ow.* Shit. A corner of his heart might have just broken off.

"We needed money."

"Right there." He pointed an index finger at her. Could she not even hear herself? *"We. As in, partners. Partners who make decisions together."*

Her eyes clouded in what looked like confusion. "It wasn't that simple. Maybe I didn't tell you because I was…afraid of what you'd do, what you'd think." Emma unclenched her fist, flexing her fingers.

"Maybe? No maybe about it. What I thought is that you decided you'd be better off with him, instead of me. So congratulations. You got your big award." Lila whimpered and Chase dropped his hands to scratch, a little too fiercely, behind her ears. "Guess you came to say you were right." After all this time, it still cut into his soul that she'd chosen Jeffries, that piece of shit wannabe cowboy, over him.

Emma hadn't believed in him. But then, she'd probably been right not to. He didn't believe in himself any more, either.

"No." She shook her head, slowly at first and then hard.

He raised his palms. "Look, it's business. I get it. I just don't happen to like the way you went about it, selling that asshole Jeffries your lyrics and then me having to hear about it from him."

"It was supposed to be a one-time thing." She didn't sound that sure.

"I don't know why you're here." Chase leaned forward, moving the dog from his lap and clasping his hands in front of him. Lila's ears perked up and, back in protection mode, she directed a sharp bark at Emma. "If you've come to say you're sorry, fine. You said it. Doesn't matter anymore." Like hell it didn't.

Emma nodded then shook her head. "Yes, I mean, no. I mean—"

"You. Said. It. You can go now."

"I can't."

"Nothing's changed.

"Everything's changed."

So could be she'd finally figured out that Jeffries wasn't much of a songwriting partner. The crap he came up with was fine for now, but would be forgettable soon enough. Well, screw that. Chase Chapman wasn't anybody's second choice. "If Jeffries isn't doing it for you and you're here to try to resurrect some kind of partnership, you can forget it."

"That's not it."

He sat back hard, the battered leather of the couch creaking in protest, and folded his arms across his chest. Arms that used to hold her so tight, he'd thought nothing could ever separate them. *Ha.* "Get to what it is, then," he said.

"Don't you deserve some of the royalties from 'Wishsome'?" She glanced around. "I'm sure you could use it."

That did it. He stood. "Your lyrics. His melody. Nothing in what that song turned out to be belongs to me. So you can take your royalties and put them—" He broke off, jamming his hands into the pockets of his jeans. "I don't want them."

"Are you writing?"

"None of your business."

"Chase—"

"I *said* none of your business." If she didn't quit looking at him like that, he was going to lose his resolve to kick her out on her beautiful butt.

"You're so incredibly talented."

"Apparently not talented enough for you to stick with me." As soon as the words were out, he regretted them, hated that he'd let her see how deeply her leaving had hurt. Sometimes the only thing a man had left was his pride and she was shooting arrows straight through his.

Her blue eyes filled. "Please. Let's talk."

"Done talking." Chase crossed the room to the front door. He opened it and waited, careful to keep his expression impassive.

She rose from the chair. "I can't leave. Not like this." Her voice sounded desperate. "Chase, please."

"You left a long time ago, Emma. Like I said, nothing is going to change that now."

She lifted her chin. "This isn't the last you'll see of me." Emma strode toward the door. When she reached it, she turned back to him. They were so close, he was afraid she could see his heart beating through his t-shirt. The damn thing was racing so fast, he was probably two seconds from passing out.

"Not everything in life is black and white," she whispered, laying a hand on his chest. "There's always another side to the story. You just have to be willing to listen to it."

Her touch was scrambling his brain like the eggs he'd made for breakfast this morning. And fuck it all—that made him furious. Another side to the story. Another...side? If he gave this woman another chance, she'd screw him all over again. And not in a good way.

She looked up at him, waiting.

This is it, Chapman. Stand up for yourself. Tell your dick to take a seat. You'll find somebody willing to take care of business without any strings. "Goodbye," he said.

Emma's expression crumpled, but only for a moment. She pulled her hand back. "Goodbye," she said. She hesitated, then walked her saucy ass straight off his porch. The teenager was gone; the woman far more dangerous.

He slammed the door and sank his back against it until he hit the floor. And he'd thought the worst problem of the day would be rebuilding the cabinets.

Thank the fuck she was gone. Out of his life again.

CHAPTER NINE

An all-consuming weariness came over Emma as she turned the car around and drove away from the house. With her fingers and toes trembling, she knew there was no way she could drive all the way back to Nashville tonight. So instead of heading for the highway, she headed for the nearby town of Maven, Ohio, and the possibility of a hotel.

With a fully stocked bar.

Not surprisingly for a small town, the streets were quiet, with few people about. A couple holding hands, walking down Main Street, their heads bent together in conversation. Just ahead of them, a man walking quickly, looking as though he had someplace to be. The lights of a bookstore, now flickering off. A gas station. Dry cleaner. A restaurant with a neon sign advertising home cooking.

On the next block, a salon with a sign announcing it the *Hair Apparent* and red daisies in pots out front, under the street lamp. At a gas station, lights blazed as a man filled the tank in his car, staring at the digital readout.

Emma had gone past a town square with a flag and a veterans' memorial before she saw a sign for a hotel. The *Earl Walker,* it said in white lights. Emma pulled the car over to look up at a faded brick building rising some six stories above the rest of the town. Most of the rooms were dark. At least someone *here* would be glad to see her.

A sigh left her body, leaving in its wake a heart bruised and bumped, but still somehow determined. This wasn't the last she'd see of Chase. She'd come too far, in miles and memories, to give up now. She'd had enough of the do-over not taken hovering around the edges of her life.

It wasn't any trouble finding a spot to park; the street was full of empty spaces. The car glided quietly to a stop in front of the brick hotel. As long as it was clean, Emma decided.

She grabbed her purse and the suitcase she'd packed so hopefully, not allowing herself to think about the fact she'd hoped to not be wearing any clothes tonight. *His loss,* she told herself, though she didn't begin to believe that.

The lobby of the Earl Walker Hotel was clean, but tattered around the edges, with paint chipped in spots at the corners, dulled wainscoting and rugs that faded into the hardwood floors. A woman about Emma's age looked up at the sound of the door, smiling from her post behind a large wooden desk. The lamp next to her seemed to be working overtime to light the whole lobby, but failing. "Hello!" the woman said brightly. She stashed the magazine she'd been reading in a drawer.

"Hi," Emma said, doing her best to muster an answering smile of her own. "Do you have a room available for the night?"

"Of course. Come right in."

"Thanks."

Emma dug in her purse to find her credit card and license, laying them on the tall, old desk, which gave off an aroma of fresh polish.

The woman tip-tapped on the computer keyboard, entering Emma's information. "Welcome to Maven," she said. "What brings you here?"

Possible responses flashed through Emma's mind before she landed on a generic, "Seeing an old friend."

"That's great." The woman smiled brightly.

It should have been. Emma sighed.

"I'm Jen." The woman extended her hand.

"Jen," Emma repeated, shaking it. "Nice to meet you."

Jen glanced at the credit card Emma had given her. "Nice to meet you, Emma. How long will you be with us?"

Good question. She'd only intended to stay the night, but now that she was here…how long might it take to reclaim a long-gone love? Chase had talked a good game, but there were moments he'd let the blustering façade slip long enough for her to see something else behind it. What that something was, she didn't know, but she wanted to find out. "A couple of days. Maybe."

Jen tipped her head. "Okay. Well, I have a nice room on our third floor. You'll love it."

Once they'd taken care of all the details, including payment, Emma found herself unlocking the door of a large room with a four-poster bed boasting white bedding and fluffy pillows and two wing chairs upholstered in a dark red. The carpet was worn to the point that little pile was left, but it was freshly vacuumed. And the bathroom, when she flipped on the light, was an eye-blinking white, from the old-fashioned pedestal sink to the tile across its floor and also forming a backsplash.

The room smelled of lavender and soap, a comforting combination. Emma opened her suitcase, but even that small motion sent a shiver of weariness through her body. Without bothering to change her clothes, she made straight for the pillows, closed her eyes, and sank into the welcoming softness of the bed.

The next thing she knew, sunlight streamed through the sheer curtains to bathe her face in light.

Emma blinked and laid an arm across her eyes. She'd slept long, hard, and without dreaming. It took a minute to process where she was. Oh, right. In Maven, Ohio. At a hotel she'd seen only in the dark. After going to talk to Chase.

Her heart pinged at the same time that, from a foot away on the bed, her phone began to vibrate. She glanced at the caller ID. *Jason.*

She couldn't talk to him now. Maybe not ever.

Instead, she burrowed further into the bedding and thought about Chase. Thought of how handsome he'd looked in the glow from the barn and how he'd looked at her, as though he'd wanted to crush her in a hug or murder her, all at the same time. But he hadn't done either. Instead he'd shut her out, closed himself off, made it clear she wasn't welcome in his life.

To hell with that.

She'd spent enough time thinking the same thing about him and all she knew now was that, as soon as she'd seen him, all of those feelings had disappeared, only to be replaced by a soul-aching, body-throbbing longing for him that left her spent.

If ever she had to be reminded that he occupied a place inside her no one else could, it had taken only one look into his dark green eyes. Fiery, intense and sensual, they had been at the heart of nearly every lyric she'd ever written.

Again, the phone vibrated. Voice mail. Emma picked it up and with a sigh, listened to Jason's voice, which started out calm and veered to tense in the span of a one-minute message. He wanted lyrics. He wanted them now. He was on a deadline.

Emma tossed the phone across the bed, where it sank into the bedding. Jason Jeffries was not her priority right now. And she couldn't begin to think about writing the lyrics to three songs when she hadn't written the lyrics to one in several years. Every time possibilities, snippets of phrases, came to her, she'd shoved them out of her mind, unwilling to think about what might have been with Chase. Where they might have gone together with those phrases.

She didn't want to go anywhere with Jason.

Half an hour later, Emma had showered and put on makeup, feeling presentable again. Her phone buzzed again, this time displaying *Taryn* in the caller ID.

"Hello?"

"Miss Zane, good morning."

"Sure. Yes. Good morning." She didn't know what to do with an assistant. There wasn't anything to assist with. That she knew of, anyway.

"Calling to go over the day's schedule with you."

Emma sank onto the bed. A schedule. The only schedule she'd ever had was put into motion by the sound of a bell echoing in the school's halls. "Is there a lot on the schedule?" she asked.

"Not too bad, ma'am." The woman's voice was brisk and professional. "I've left you plenty of downtime to work on the songs Mr. Jeffries has been calling about."

Everyone knew about those damn songs.

"Now, today at noon—"

"Taryn," Emma interrupted. "Please cancel everything I have scheduled for the next few days."

"Everything?" her assistant squeaked.

"Yes." This was a new voice, one that expected to be obeyed. "I'm out of town. I'll let you know when I'm on the way back."

"Oh." Taryn recovered quickly. "Yes, ma'am. I understand."

"Good." There was that snippy voice again. Emma made sure she softened it and then added, "Thank you. Oh, and Taryn?"

"Yes. Right here."

"You're doing…a great job."

Emma could have sworn she heard pencil lead snap on the other end of the line. "Thank you. Ma'am."

Schedule cleared, without Emma having to make a single apology. *Nice*.

Emma was surprised, after descending to the ground floor in a creaky elevator, to see Jen at the front desk again, looking cheerful in a bright yellow top. The sounds of Michael Bublé came from a CD player beside her.

"Good morning!" Jen called. A white-haired couple at the other end of the lobby, dressed in matching Ohio University shirts, turned to look.

Emma nodded at them. Her empty stomach rumbled on cue and she turned back to Jen. "Good morning. Is there a restaurant somewhere close?"

Leaning across the desk in her eagerness to please, Jen gave her directions to one a few blocks down. It featured, the woman swore, the best blueberry pancakes Emma would ever eat.

Once the prospect was embedded in her mind, Emma couldn't wait. She walked out of the large, heavy doors to the Earl Walker and outside, turning left as Jen had instructed.

Outside, the air was already beginning to warm, carrying on a small breeze the scent of flowers. They were everywhere on Main Street, hanging in baskets from lampposts and planted in pots in front of storefronts. Balancing on the bed of a small truck, a man in shorts wielded a large hose, spraying water into each basket as the truck crept along the street. He looked away to nod a curious hello at Emma and then turned back to his work.

She walked by the salon she'd seen the night before. The door opened abruptly, with a clang of bells and a woman with dark, short hair, red lipstick and large red earrings walked out to drop a sandwich board on the cement of the sidewalk. *It's better hair*, the sign read. Emma couldn't help it; she cringed at the pun.

The woman caught her expression and narrowed her eyes. "Mornin'," she said.

"Good morning," Emma replied politely, and continued on.

She smelled the blueberry pancakes a block away from the restaurant and by the time she reached it, she felt ravenous. Inside, most tables in the small place were already taken. It was a hum of activity, with orders being called out from the kitchen, plates clanking and people laughing, their voices rumbling in conversation.

A waitress near the door motioned in the direction of an empty table. "Have a seat, hon," she called. "Be right with you."

Emma obeyed, sitting down next to the table of a very pregnant woman and a man with his hand over hers. They glanced at her with a flash of pleasant smiles.

A waitress appeared before Emma long enough to slide a menu encased in plastic in front of her, flip a mug onto the table, and slosh coffee into it. Apparently, in this restaurant, everyone drank coffee. Emma opened her mouth to say something, but thought better of it. Besides, she needed coffee this morning. She took a sip.

The couple next to her was deep in conversation. "I don't understand," the pregnant woman said. "He loves playing with the band. I can tell. When he's playing, he gets this expression where he looks like he's somewhere else. Somewhere good."

Emma took another slow sip. She knew that look. She knew the feeling of being transported by the music to a better place. A place where all the pain, the hurts, the joys of the day just rolled into one and you felt as though they were made bearable somehow by the melody that carried you on it, the words that spoke to a part of you deep inside.

Crazy. She shook her head, realizing how silly it was to let an overheard snippet of conversation to take her somewhere these people didn't even have in mind. She had music on the brain; she had Chase on the brain.

"He says he doesn't want to, anymore," the man said. "Nothing I can do about that." Emma caught a flash of a gold band on his finger as he raised his hand to run it through his hair.

"It's a woman. I know it's some woman who's done this to him," his wife replied.

"Beth, he hasn't even played with us that many times—"

"But he's been out with us a bunch of times." She made a clucking noise with her tongue. "He's drinking too much, I know he is, and he won't talk about it. I can't believe he smashed all of those cabinets, after the work he put into them. Something bad is going on with him." She shook her head. "And now he's going to give up something he likes doing, which is playing with your band, and all he'll do is spend more time alone."

Poor guy. Sweet of these people to be so concerned about him, but Emma guessed that's what small-town people did. Got all up into everyone's business. Those blueberry pancakes smelled really, really good. Emma looked around for the waitress. She hoped she didn't have to wait too long. Now that she thought about it, it had been at least twenty-four hours since she'd last eaten. No wonder her stomach was protesting its treatment.

"The way he bolted out of the bar after that song came on." The pregnant woman continued, shaking her head. "Why? It's just a song, a song that's been on the radio about a million times."

"I asked him about that, Beth. He just said it sounded familiar."

"Familiar." Pregnant Beth snorted and took a drink of her orange juice. "I don't buy that. He looked like he was about to kill someone when it came on."

"That's what I said to him."

She set her glass down. "I'll bet it has to do with the woman who broke his heart. The song had to have triggered something."

Songs did that. Were *meant* to do that. Only the really good ones succeeded.

"We don't know he's had his heart broken," the man said.

"I know. I can tell."

The waitress slid to a stop on her roller sneakers at Emma's table. "What can I get you?"

She had just opened her mouth to order when Beth's husband spoke again, fervently this time. "You can't worry this much about Chase. He can take care of himself. What he does with his time isn't our business."

Emma's mouth snapped shut. *Chase*. What were the odds of more than one Chase in this area? Zero. She passed the menu to the waitress. "Blueberry pancakes," she whispered.

Gum snapped. "Regular blueberry or whole wheat blueberry?"

"Doesn't matter."

"Real butter or I Can't Believe It's Not Butter?"

"Doesn't *matter*."

The waitress glided away. Emma scooted her chair a few inches closer to the couple, careful not to stare.

"He's miserable," Beth said. "We're his friends and we have to help him. That makes it our business."

"He's a nice guy, but he mostly keeps to himself. He plays in my band, or at least he did, when we have a gig. That doesn't give us the right to make him tell us all about it whenever he has some kind of a problem," her husband said, but he sounded weary, as though he knew he was losing this battle.

"Not us. He needs a woman. A woman he can talk to."

I couldn't agree more, Beth. And I know just the woman.

CHAPTER TEN

"Beth." The husband's voice carried a warning. "He doesn't want to be fixed up."

Another long sip of orange juice. "He might not think he does," Beth answered. "But neither did you."

"Aw, come on, now, that was different."

"No, it wasn't. And look at you now. Happily married and about to become a daddy. You think Chase doesn't deserve that kind of happiness?"

Emma locked her eyes on a table closer to the center of the restaurant that had several gray-haired men sitting around it, each staring down into a coffee cup he cradled. But her attention was riveted on the table right next to her and the pregnant woman looking to fix up Chase.

"Yeah, but he would have seen just about every eligible woman in this town already, and if he was interested he would have done something about it by now."

Relief sagged Emma's body and she had to fight to keep back her smile. Chase hadn't dated anyone here. She wasn't competing for his attention. *Yet.* She took another drink of her coffee.

"So we import someone, Carl," Beth persisted. "Angela has a sister in Athens who's single."

"Angela, the one who can't ever stop talking?"

Ha, Emma thought triumphantly. Chase would hate that.

"That doesn't mean her sister is the same. Besides, I've seen a picture of her. She's beautiful."

"I don't know," Carl sighed.

That's right, Carl. Tell her it's a bad idea. Chase doesn't want to meet Angela's sister.

"I'm not saying she's the one for him. But what if she is? We have to do something about that."

Back off, Beth.

A plate of steaming blueberry pancakes appeared before her, along with silverware and the waitress's rushed, "There you go."

"Thanks," Emma whispered, unwilling to interrupt her eavesdropping.

"If this is about the business, there are plenty of other people you can fix up."

Business? She must have heard wrong.

"I can't believe you would think that." Beth sounded offended. "This is about our friend."

"Okay, okay. You might be right," Carl said, sounding resigned.

Don't give in, Carl!

"But he would be a great one to start things off with."

"Beth!"

"I'm only saying."

"More coffee?" the waitress asked Emma.

Emma shook her head. The waitress took the hint.

"Fine," Carl said. "But you're going to be the one explaining it to him."

"Not a problem. So I'll call Angela and find out how to reach her sister."

Her *beautiful* sister. An urgency rose in Emma's throat that had her talking before she even knew she was. "Excuse me?" she said to the two, who were gathering their things to leave, having come to a decision on Chase's future as a husband and father.

Beth turned a friendly, seventy-five-watt smile on Emma. "Yes? Hi."

"Hi," Emma said.

Carl turned in his chair to also look at her.

"I hope I'm not intruding, but I was just wondering…I'm new in town and wondered if you could recommend….um…." *What?* "A hair salon?" Beth was going to see right through this one.

If she did, she didn't let on. "Sure, of course," Beth said. "*Hair Apparent*, right downtown. That's where everybody goes."

"Thanks!" Emma said brightly. "That's helpful. It's hard when you, um, don't know people."

A tiny furrow appeared between Beth's brows.

Emma forged ahead. "And do you know places that might be okay for a, you know, single girl to go out by herself?"

"Depends," Beth and her husband said at the same time. Beth looked at her husband, her expression clearly conveying she would take it from here. He closed his mouth and leaned back in his chair.

"A single girl. Are you wanting to meet someone?" Beth asked. "Or be left alone?"

Emma dropped her gaze, wondering how far she could take this. Then she thought about Chase being set up with Angela's sister and decided she could take it as far as she needed to. "Well, yes, I guess so. Meet someone, I mean. At least—I would be open to it." She could feel her cheeks pinking, helping to make her case. "It can get lonely, not knowing many people."

Carl looked at his wife. "Isn't this what you need? She would be great for—"

"Shhh!" she scolded him. He folded his arms across his chest.

"I'm Beth," she said, extending her hand.

"Emma." She took Beth's hand in hers and shook.

Carl perked up then to offer his own hand and his name.

"When are you due? Your first?" Emma asked Beth.

"Two weeks and four days. Not soon enough! And yes, she'll be our first."

"Congratulations."

"Thank you. We're excited and we'll probably be those annoying new parents who show off all of the pictures, every chance we get. Birth through high school. Don't you just hate that? But it's so us." She gestured to herself and Carl. "Emma, where are you from?"

Emma blinked at the rapid change in subject, but didn't miss a step. "The Pacific Northwest."

"That's a long way. What brings you to Maven?"

"Beth—" Carl protested. He was silenced with a look.

"It's okay," Emma rushed to say, which gave her a few seconds to think about how to reply. "I'm a teacher," she said. And left it at that. Let Beth draw her own conclusions.

Beth leaned forward on one elbow, cupping her chin in her hand. "*Are* you? That's really interesting."

Carl watched his wife.

Emma watched his wife.

Beth, her head now tipped to one side, watched Emma. "It *must* be hard not knowing people."

Emma nodded then put a self-conscious hand to her hair. The bangs, swept to one side, were too long for her liking; they kept flopping into her eyes. Maybe a visit to the hair salon wouldn't be such a bad idea, after all.

"I just had an idea. You might think I'm crazy, seeing as we've only just met—"

"Oh no, not at all," Emma rushed to say.

"But I hate to see anyone be alone."

"That's true," Carl snorted to himself, fingering his napkin.

"There's a place in town that's pretty fun. Has good music, anyway, even if the beer isn't always that cold. Maybe you'd want to meet us there tonight for something to eat. I could introduce you around."

"Around?" Emma was afraid to hope.

"No pressure or anything." Beth seemed to be making a concerted effort to keep her voice light. "But I might know someone for you to meet."

Carl turned to Emma. "She loves to fix people up. You were sunk when you said you'd be open to it."

"Hey!" His wife playfully slapped his hand. "Don't pay any attention to him."

"It's okay. I *did* say I would be open to it." She hesitated and then asked, "Would you be fixing me up with anyone in particular?" She bit down on her lip. *Too direct.*

Beth didn't seem to think so. She surveyed Emma, all business. "Well, let's see. What do you like to do for fun?"

"Music."

"Listen to it or play it?"

"Both. I'm, well, a music teacher." Right now, she felt like a semi-interesting bug, squirming under Beth's microscope.

"A music teacher." Beth stroked her chin, contemplating. "Good, very good. Go ahead. What else do you like?"

She took a deep breath. "Long hikes to high-up places. Dogs. Movies that make me cry. Books that make me laugh. Because if I cry too much, my nose starts to run and I get all—" What was she *saying*? Beth was going to think she was too crazy to be set up with *anyone*, let alone Chase. She took a breath and regrouped. "Skiing. Snow. Sand at the beach. Spicy food. Roller coasters."

Carl looked at her sideways, one eyebrow raised.

"Well, not all at once, of course." Emma looked down. Her pancakes had turned cold, the syrup congealing on the top.

Beth practically swatted at her own words to keep them from getting too excited. "Really? What would your ideal guy be like?"

"That's easy," Carl said before Emma could answer. "He'd come skiing down a mountain holding a jalapeno pizza, a guitar, a dog, a box of Kleenex and tickets to Cedar Point."

Beth chortled, one hand on her round tummy. "Honey, you're doing so much better at listening. I'm proud of you."

"Cedar Point?" Emma asked.

"Roller coasters in Sandusky, overlooking the water," Beth answered. "They go crazy high. Carl loves 'em."

"I do," he agreed.

"You are not taking our child on one of those."

"Watch me." Carl grinned.

Beth frowned.

"Um, so… back to…?" Emma ventured.

"Right." Beth reached into her purse and pulled out a piece of paper and a pen. She wrote something on the paper and handed it to Carl, who handed it to Emma. "The place is called Gil's. It's not too far, but you have to know how to get there. These are the directions and I've put my cell number down, in case you get lost or anything." She put both palms on the table, ready to push herself away. "I have a call to make. This will be fun! Won't it, Carl?"

"Fun," he repeated.

"Okay. Tonight." Emma's mind raced as she tried to remember whether she'd thrown any clothes into that overnight bag that she could wear to a place called Gil's.

"Don't get dressed up or anything. It's a bar."

Beth must have read her mind. "Okay." She hoped it would be Chase Beth invited. It *had* to be Chase. "Can you tell me the name of the person you…you know, have in mind for me to meet?"

"He's adorable. A musician, just like you. His name is Chase. I can't promise he'll be there, but he's never yet said no to me on anything." She paused. "And this isn't the time to start."

"Sounds great." Emma's heart began pinging with excitement, even as she realized that Chase was going to kill her for this. And then Beth would know it had been a ruse to get him in a setting where he had to be nice to her. She should just hop in her car and drive back to Nashville. *Now.*

She opened her mouth but didn't get a chance to say anything before Beth added, "Oh, one more thing. And I hope you don't think it's weird or anything." She turned a hopeful smile on Emma. "It's just that there *might* be a video camera there tonight. For a little bit."

Ohh-kaay. "Why?"

"I'm going to start my own business. Because, the thing is, I've introduced so many people who wouldn't otherwise ever have thought of getting together. I still can't quite get my head around the thought of anyone actually paying me to do it, but people keep telling me they would."

"Everybody wants Beth to fix them up," Carl added, his chest puffing out. Then he glanced at his wife. "Everybody who *wants* to be fixed up, anyway."

She ignored him. "So for promotion, a website, the whole deal, we want to get a video of a couple when they meet for the first time."

Uh-oh.

"It's crazy to think about, but kind of fun, too. You know what I mean?"

Emma opened her mouth to come clean, or at least back out, but Beth ran right over her.

"Carl was the one who thought of a name for the business. Tell her, Carl. Go ahead."

He looked sheepish, but proud. "Matches Made in Maven."

"Isn't that great?" Beth beamed. "Do you love it? Carl might even pitch it to a TV producer. He has such big ideas."

"Beth, I don't think—"

"Oh, don't worry!" Beth hastened to assure her. "No pressure. If it doesn't work out, it's fine. Just fine."

"Except that it usually always works out when Beth has her hand in it," Carl said.

"Look at you," his wife said, giving him a quick kiss on the cheek. "I could swear that a few minutes ago, you were telling me I shouldn't do this."

He frowned. "Oh, yeah. I was."

"No backing out now," she told him. Then she turned her attention to Emma. "Not that I'm charging for this introduction, because I'm not. This one is on the house because you're doing me a big favor. And we'll stay out of your way. You won't even notice the camera, I promise."

The camera might notice the thunderclouds on Chase's face when he saw Emma. On the other hand, Carl had said things always worked out when Beth was involved. That was a chance worth taking. Emma struggled with what to say, before finally settling for, "Thank you."

She was going to hell for lying; she was sure of it now. At least she'd probably know people there.

"You're welcome," Beth said, straightening with some difficulty, given the extra passenger she carried. "We'll see you tonight. Come on, Carl."

After they'd gone, Emma took hungry bites of her cold pancakes. Then she switched to staring at the piece of paper with the address and directions to Gil's, plus Beth's phone number. Apprehension about what Chase would say and do when he saw her pooled in her tummy and began creeping its way upward. She set her fork on the table. Only one thing to do.

Shove it all out of her mind with a trip to the hair salon.

CHAPTER ELEVEN

In the hair salon, "Let it Snow" was on the CD player, with the singers calling for frightful weather, despite the summer heat building outside. Over the whirr of a blow dryer, three stylists chatted with the customers in their chairs and a bored mom rocked a baby in a car seat with her foot and waited her turn, flipping through the pages of a magazine.

A small, thin woman standing at the chair closest to the door called out to Emma as soon as she walked in. "Hi!" she said, in a voice loud enough to belong to someone twice her size. It was the woman Emma had seen putting the sign out earlier.

Scissors flashed in the sunlight as she snipped the red hair of her customer. "Have an appointment?" She was wearing a smock with Christmas elves on it.

Emma glanced back outside. Still summer. "No. I—Are you all booked up?"

"We can fit you in. No problem." She turned to shout over one shoulder. "Chrissy!"

A woman who looked to be in her early twenties appeared from the back. "I'm here."

"Would you check the book to see who can help this lady?" Her customer reached up to brush red hair from her eyes as the scissors again swished over her head.

Chrissy scooted to the reception desk, her shiny dark hair bouncing. Her expression flickered between a grimace and a smile. "What are you looking to have done?" she asked Emma.

"Just a trim. These bangs are too long. They're driving me crazy."

Both of them peered down at the penciled appointments for the day. "Okay, we could—"

"I will do it."

The voice at Emma's side appeared to come from out of nowhere. And it spoke in a *very* familiar accent.

Emma's neck snapped up so fast, she could have done muscle damage. It *couldn't* be.

It was. Now with her hair dyed silver, complete with blue highlights. But still the same eyes, the same voice, the same leopard-print heels, and the same violent red lipstick. "Are you fucking kidding me?" Emma breathed.

"You have come for an appointment, have you not?" Madame Claire asked.

Chrissy paused, pencil in hand, to stare at the two of them. "Umm, Claire is new," she said, as if that explained everything. Or even anything.

"She was here before me." Emma gestured frantically at the mom with the baby, who didn't even look up.

"She's waiting for Rachel," Chrissy said, sounding apologetic.

"And you are here for me, are you not?" A bony finger beckoned her closer. "You will come." Madame Claire turned and began marching down the row of chairs, leaving no room for argument.

Emma's startled gaze met Chrissy's.

"I'll keep an eye on you," Chrissy whispered.

"Thanks," Emma whispered back. Then she followed the psychic's retreating back to the last station in the row.

Once Emma had taken a seat, feet on the floor instead of the footrests in case she needed to make a fast escape, Madame Claire whipped a plastic cape over her with unnecessary flourish, snapping it in place at the neck.

"This is a surprise," Emma said.

"All of life, it is so."

Emma spotted a paper sign taped to the mirror. *Hair by Claire. If you dare.* She pointed. So you're a hairdresser now."

"I can do many things. Too bad you did not know this." Madame Claire picked up a pair of scissors and stared at them, as though looking for instructions.

"Really. Many things."

"That is what I said. Yes."

Emma dropped her voice. "Maybe my do-over isn't one of them. It's not going so well. Everything is all screwed up."

Madame Claire lifted a section of Emma's bangs, holding the hair between her fingers.

"It is distressing to hear this."

"Not as distressing as it is to live it."

Further inspection of the bangs, which weren't all that complicated. "There is, of course, no guarantee. Or money back. For that you find Wal-Mart, yes?"

Emma gripped the arms of the chair tight. "I didn't ask for a guarantee. But if you're really a psychic, as you claim to be, you would have to know how it would go." The woman in the next chair turned to look. Emma gave her a weak smile and never-mind wave before refocusing on the image of Madame Claire reflected in the mirror.

Madame Claire met Emma's gaze and then averted her eyes. "There *might*, it is possible, have been something missing in the spell. Or not. One does not truly know."

Emma gaped. "Missing?"

"As I said, one cannot know for sure."

"*Missing?*" This time, Emma's voice had ratcheted up to a screech. Heads turned.

"Please. To keep your voice down. I must have quiet when I work."

"I–" Emma shook her head, words failing her. "I suppose you came here to tell me that. How did you even know this is where I would be?"

"You think I cannot be a psychic and a worker of hair magic at the same time? Hmm?"

Before Emma had a chance to answer, Chrissy appeared at her side. "Would you like me to shampoo her for you, Claire?"

"You think the shampoo I cannot do?" Madame Claire's eyebrows climbed.

Chrissy kept her expression blank. "Of course not, but I'm the shampoo girl, so you know…"

"Well," the silver-haired psychic huffed. "Then you shall take her and apply the shampoo."

"Yes, I shall," Chrissy murmured. She motioned to Emma. "Please follow me."

As Madame Claire busied herself with inspecting the tools at her station, Emma went with Chrissy to the shampoo bowl, laying her head back against the towel placed under her neck for comfort even as her mind spun with the news that the spell might have been performed wrong. That her life might have been upended, her heart wrenched by Chase yet again, because of a mistake.

"Claire is new," Chrissy explained. "Walked in this morning and my mother hired her on the spot. We had two stylists quit last week and she was a little panicked."

"Oh," Emma replied, unsure whether she should admit to knowing the psychic, or not. "Is your mom the one who spoke to me, the one with the, um…?"

"Christmas smock. Yes."

Warm water streamed across Emma's head. A squirt of cold shampoo and Chrissy was massaging her scalp with practiced hands. It felt good, really good. And the shampoo smelled of coconut and mango, making her think of a warm beach and cold ocean.

"She's a little crazy."

The beach image disappeared with a pop. "Yes," Emma agreed fervently. Then she realized Chrissy might not be talking about Madame Claire. "I mean—"

"Christmas music is her favorite, so she doesn't see why she can't listen to it all year. Do you know what it's like to be a kid playing outside in hundred-degree heat while your mom is blasting 'Frosty the Snowman'?"

Emma bit back a laugh. "Let me guess. Refreshing?"

"No. Really not."

"Could be worse things than Christmas music."

"Don't think so. I learned to count by singing 'The Twelve Days of Christmas.' Didn't believe for a long time that there were any numbers that came after twelve. What did you get for them? There had to be something. Thirteen therapists a-therapying?"

Emma laughed.

Chrissy escalated the pressure of her fingers, and Emma shoved the thought of Madame Claire from her mind long enough to let her body relax. She tried to pull the beach image back, but the tide must have gone out. The image was gone.

Chrissy kept talking above her. When she paused, her voice lifted in what sounded like a question, Emma responded, "Mmmm?"

"I said, there's no big rush, right? But my mother says her sister is going to be a great-grandmother before she's ever a grandmother and that it's just wrong. It's all about her, it always is. Just because she was married at seventeen doesn't mean I'm washed up at twenty-two."

"That has to be tough to deal with," Emma murmured. The soothing effects of the scalp massage were beginning to make their way down through her body, until even her toes felt like Jell-O. *Madame who?*

"It is. And not only do I have to work for her, I have to live with her. "

Emma made a sound of sympathy. "Your mother doesn't get it. You don't have to marry someone to be happy."

"Never said I wasn't happy." Chrissy's fingers stilled.

"I understand." But she'd give anything not to.

"I probably am."

"You probably are."

The massage resumed. When Chrissy spoke again, her voice sounded dreamy and far away. "There is one guy I'm interested in. But he doesn't even look at me. Not like, you know, a guy would who's interested in someone. *That* way."

"You should talk to Beth," Emma said, drowsiness wrapping her in its soft edges. "She seems to know everyone."

"Pregnant Beth? Married to Carl?"

"Mmmm."

"Yeah, I don't know. That hasn't done me any good so far."

"Matchmaker." Emma made an effort to form a complete sentence. "She fixed me up, for tonight."

"That was fast."

Warm water poured over her hair again. Next came the conditioner, which Chrissy gently wove through her strands. Emma didn't want to get up. She just wanted to lay here and take a nap, Jell-O toes and all.

"Who's the guy?"

"You wouldn't know him."

Chrissy rinsed out the conditioner, wrung out Emma's wet hair, and wrapped her head in a warm towel. "What's his name?"

She knew she shouldn't say. It was so iffy, this whole thing with Beth and Carl tonight. Chase might not even show. Or Beth might decide to set her up with someone else and leave Chase in the hands of Angela's beautiful sister.

Ow. Trampoline stomach. What if he liked Angela's sister? What if Emma never got him back and this screwed up do-over was some sort of punishment for her being too scared to trust Chase in the first place?

The familiar setting of the hair salon confessional took over and Emma found herself whispering his name to Chrissy, as though saying it out loud, could, in itself, make it happen. "Chase."

"Chase."

Something in her voice caused an alarm bell to trill in Emma's brain. She curled her fingers around the arms of the chair and sat up, her head wobbling from the weight of the towel. "Don't tell me you know him. How small is this town?" She tried and failed a laugh.

"Maybe."

"Oh."

"I mean, I mentioned him to Beth, but nothing happened. Guess he wasn't interested. Or she just didn't want to set me up with him." Chrissy's casual tone sounded too deliberate. Emma wasn't fooled. Great. Chase *would* have to be the guy Chrissy liked.

"He's probably not that great, anyway." *Ha.*

"You haven't met him yet." Two spots of red appeared on the other woman's cheeks and her shoulders turned inward.

Emma was at a loss. She didn't want to feel sorry for Chrissy, even though she did, and she didn't want to get any deeper into a story that wasn't true.

She only wanted her bangs to quit getting caught on her eyelashes, making her every blink an event.

"Let's get you back to Claire's station." Chrissy removed the towel and began gently pulling a comb through Emma's wet hair.

Madame Claire was nowhere to be seen.

"Have you thought about moving somewhere else?" Emma asked.

"What, and leave all this?" Chrissy swept her hand to encompass the salon. "Give up the chance to take over my mother's salon one day?" She sighed. "She has it all planned out for me."

"What do you *want* to be doing?" In her purse, Emma's phone began ringing. She ignored it. Probably Jason, who didn't believe in no news being good news. In this case, he was right. "If you could choose anything."

Chrissy bent so her hair would cover part of her face, again concentrating on the task at hand.

"Come on," Emma said. "You can tell me."

Chrissy straightened and looked away. She twisted her mouth and then finally said, "Sing."

"Sing? What's wrong with that?"

"Sssh! My mother will hear you."

Emma glanced in the salon owner's direction. Her customer was gone and Chrissy's mother was humming to "I'll be Home for Christmas" as she swept up her station. Emma lowered her voice. "So why don't you sing, then?"

"Can't count on making enough to live."

A part of Emma's heart squeezed tight at hearing nearly the same words she'd said not all that long ago. She channeled Chase to say the words he'd said to her. "You'll never know unless you try."

"Yeah, that's okay for other people. Not me."

"Have you sung in front of anyone?"

"Not unless you count my cat. The thought of singing in front of people makes me want to pass out. I couldn't even do it with the church choir."

Emma's phone started ringing again. It was likely her imagination, but it seemed to have taken on a new level of urgency. Jason had to be getting more desperate.

"Come to this place we're going to tonight," she heard herself say. "Gil's."

"Why?" Chrissy asked. She looked perplexed.

"Why not?"

"You afraid to meet this guy?"

"No. Yes." Emma exhaled. "Maybe."

"He's great."

"I know. I mean—I don't know. But if you came, the band might let you sing a song with them and then you'd know whether you're any good and just as importantly, whether you like performing. Your cat's not going to tell you the truth." She sighed. "If you don't take the chance, you'll regret it. Trust me."

"Don't think so." Chrissy's hands sliced through the air in the universal sign of no. "Told you. I'd pass out."

Emma leaned back in the chair, out of the danger zone. "No, you won't. I won't let you." And how exactly would she do that?

"I couldn't."

Emma pounced on the doubt she heard. "Fine. Stay here. Live the dream. One shampoo at a time."

The other woman dipped her head, staring at the floor. "People might laugh. Or even worse, they'd try not to laugh."

"So what. You won't die. Even Pink says that." *Who* was speaking here? Madame Claire's do-over must have included a personality overhaul. Emma Zane was, above all, *not* a risk taker.

Yet, in the space of a couple of days, she'd run away from a comfortable new life, blown off her only visible source of income, confronted her former boyfriend, invented a lie to get a date under false pretenses with said former boyfriend, and invited a not-unattractive younger woman with a crush on him to join her on that date.

Hell, at this rate, she could actually get the guy for once, in a flurry of sunshine, hearts and forever happiness, screwed-up spell, or not. Or she could end up alone, broke and pointlessly suing Madame Claire for breach of do-over.

One or the other.

At this point, Emma wasn't betting on the former.

CHAPTER TWELVE

"That is enough," Madame Claire commanded Chrissy. She had moved to the salon station on cat feet, not making a sound. Fairly impressive, considering she still wore the leopard-print heels. "You will leave now."

Chrissy started to do as she'd been told. Then she ducked back and whispered to Emma, "I'll think about it."

"Shoo!" Madame Claire flicked her fingers at Chrissy.

"Still a model of charm, I see," Emma observed.

Madame Claire picked up Emma's bangs and combed through them again with a critical eye. "What is it that girl will think about?"

"Never mind that. I want to talk about what's happened. There has to be a reason you think something's missing from the—" She dropped her voice. "Spell."

"My mother. That is what she thinks. Not that she has been asked. But her opinion, she gives it. No matter."

Seemed to be a mother/daughter theme going today. "Did she tell you how to fix it?"

Snip went the scissors. A wisp of hair fell into Emma's lap.

"It was three in the morning. Maybe I listen, maybe I do not."

"Call her."

Another snip of the scissors. "You do not understand. She only talks to me at three in the morning. When the line, it is available."

Emma realized, not for the first time, that a conversation with Madame Claire made her head hurt. "Get her a calling card or a different phone plan so she can call you any time."

The sound that came out of Madame Claire was a combination of snort, bark and sneeze. It took a few seconds for Emma to realize it was supposed to be a laugh.

"Very funny you are. My mother, she has been dead for five years. A calling card. Please."

Emma put a hand to her temple to rub it at the same time Madame Claire took another snip with the scissors.

She heard a muttered exclamation that sounded like a curse word. In a different language. Alarmed, Emma asked, "What is it?"

Her bangs were fluffed, rearranged and then fluffed some more. Hair wisps were brushed from her cape to the floor. "It is nothing."

Emma wasn't sure she believed her, but decided to go back to the dead mother calling. Because a person who wasn't on the planet any more couldn't have a valid opinion about a spell gone wrong, right? She needed that to be right. "How can your mother call you if she has passed away?"

"Only when the line it is available, I said to you. There are many waiting to make such a call." Madame Claire shrugged. "Of course, most do not *take* the call. That is their miss."

"Loss."

"As you wish."

"But you take the call. You talk to your mother."

"Some talk. Lots of argue."

"And she told you something was missing when you did that spell."

"Ah, that." Madame Claire clucked her tongue. "We shall see." She leaned down, closer to Emma's ear. "Tell me, do you remember your life before you came to see me? The life before the do-over?"

"Of course I do."

"That is the trouble," Madame Claire said sadly. "You are not to. It was also such with your friend. My mother, she is of the mind that I did not say all of the words I was to say. *Now* she is to tell me."

No small miracle that the psychic's mother had a mind to think that, given that she was allegedly…dead and all. A mother's ability to scold must continue into the afterlife. Not good news.

Even as she pondered this, Emma flashed back to the phone conversation she'd overheard in Tensley's bookstore. Her friend had demanded a promise that Madame Claire would "get it right this time." Her stomach turned over. Emma's was the second do-over gone wrong.

She pulled her shoulders back, hoping to assert some sort of control over the situation. "So what does this all mean?" she asked.

"It means you are caused to believe your"—Madame Claire looked to the right and to the left, where stylists were busy chatting with their clients—"do-over is not to your satisfaction."

Realization dawned on Emma. "Because if I didn't know that I'd been *given* a do-over, I wouldn't know it wasn't turning out right." She lowered her voice, but picked up speed as her sense of injustice grew. "I wouldn't even know this is a second chance, is that what you're saying? I would think this is the way things had always been, that I had never *not* gone to Nashville."

Madame Claire turned Emma's chair away from the mirror. "This, it is the problem. As I have said. I made the changes. All was to be well. But my mother, she will not stop with the talking." She raised her arm in the air, scissors flashing in the light. "All the night, she will not stop the talking. Most probably why I did not say all the words, *if* I did not say all the words. Tired. Do you understand? Tired of arguing in the night. She should call someone else maybe sometime."

"Or maybe you should try listening to her," Emma said between clenched teeth.

The other woman made a non-committal sound, lifting a shoulder. "Perhaps. Perhaps not." She pulled a length of Emma's hair away from her head, examining the ends. She opened the scissors.

"No!" Emma said. She still wasn't sure about her bangs; she wasn't about to let the bumbling psychic loose on trimming her ends.

Madame Claire frowned.

"Just blow dry it."

"As you wish."

Emma grabbed the woman's arm. "But it's *not* as I wish. That's the whole point. He doesn't even want anything to do with me. I was better off before when I could wonder about what could have been, instead of what *is*. Don't you get it?"

Madame Claire picked up a pink blow dryer and turned it over in her hands. Then she turned to Emma. "I do, as you say, get it." She pronounced *it* as *eet*. "But do you understand that what you must now do is change his mind."

"I'm trying. Believe me, I'm trying."

"You must keep trying. I will help." The blow dryer roared to life and the psychic-turned-hairdresser aimed it straight at Emma's head. Her hair scattered in every direction while Emma bent her head, thinking. Tonight, she had to get Chase to talk to her, really talk to her. She'd hurt him. She would have to make it up to him, get him to see her as the person she really was, not the one who ordered around assistants and thought of herself as some big Nashville deal.

She sighed. After a few minutes, she realized Madame Claire was still only blowing her hair around, not doing any styling. She lifted her head just as the woman put the dryer down and began brushing her hair, moving it in one direction and then the other.

"You are done," Madame Claire announced.

Emma put her foot down and tried to spin the chair toward the mirror. Madame Claire held on to the arms, preventing it. "Let me see," Emma protested.

"It is very nice you look. You will pay now."

As Emma rose from the chair, several things happened at once. She turned on her heel to see the mirror reflect a wildly poufed-out version of her hair, looking a lot like a hairball her cat had once coughed up. At the same time, Chrissy came running toward the chair, tripping over her apologies for being tied up with another client and Chrissy's mother stopped singing mid-carol to shout, "Claire!"

Everyone in the salon stared at Emma. She stared at her reflection. Madame Claire patted the back of Emma's hair and then let her hand drop, murmuring to herself. She leaned forward to whisper in Emma's ear, under the cover of "Santa Claus is Coming to Town," "It is not actually a worker of hair magic I am."

"It is not," Emma whispered back. She saw the woman wring her bejeweled hands and a pang of sympathy went through her. Madame Claire's dead mother would no doubt have something to say about this, too.

Emma straightened. "What's the matter?" she asked, looking around the shop. "I saw this exact style in *Vogue* last week. Mad— *Claire* did a great job of copying it. I love it." Nothing that a shower and shampoo wouldn't take care of.

"Oh," said Chrissy's mother.

"Oh," said one befuddled client and then another. "*Vogue*," said a third.

Chrissy squinted, possibly hoping a less focused view would be more flattering.

Madame Claire recovered to say, "You shall pay now," and begin striding toward the reception desk, silver hair shining and leopard heels tapping.

Emma followed her, hairball head held high.

Before Chrissy reached the desk to check her out, Madame Claire leaned in and whispered, "I will say thank you."

"No tip," Emma said under her breath.

"But the— *Vogue?*"

"No tip."

"As you wish."

***

Chase stood outside Gil's, hands jammed in the pockets of his jeans. He was late, mostly because he'd climbed in and out of his truck six times, started it and circled back twice, idled for several minutes and then slammed it back into drive and shown up here. Now he couldn't pull the trigger and go inside. *Shit.*

He didn't want to meet whoever Beth had in mind for him, did not want to be fixed up. He was only here because Carl had reminded him of the times Beth had gone out of her way to make Chase dinner. *And* she was pregnant after years of trying and Chase didn't want to do anything that might upset and send her into early labor. He knew Carl worried about that.

Not that Chase knew anything about what would send someone into labor, but he wasn't going to take the chance. Carl and Beth were his friends and they were good people. Wasn't something to take lightly.

Yet, here he was. Unable to go inside. He kicked at the dirt with the toe of his shoe. If Emma hadn't come to see him, he wouldn't be having this problem. He could have walked inside and not given a fuck. Might even have had some kind of connection with whoever Beth had in there waiting for him.

Seeing Emma had brought back every memory, shot every feeling for her back up to the surface, where it lit up and burned him like smoldering ash. The feel of her body, soft and curved, against his. Her hair, getting caught in his whiskers, her full lips closing on his, her round breasts with their pink nipples fitting perfectly in his hands. He'd come with her in ways he never had since and the realization filled him with an intense longing he refused to give in to.

She'd betrayed him; gone behind his back. That he couldn't forgive. That he'd *never* forgive.

"Chase."

He looked up. It was Carl, standing just outside the entrance to Gil's, a huge look of relief on his face. "Man, I was afraid you weren't coming," Carl said. He was at Chase's side in a few strides, clapping a large hand on his back. "That would've been tough on Beth."

"I said I would, so I'm here." No point in mentioning the number of false starts it had taken to get him here.

"Thanks, man. And hey this girl, she's hot. Shouldn't be a bad night. At. All."

"I'm not staying long. I'll meet her, buy her a drink and get out. I've got shit to do."

"Okay, okay. No problem." Carl kept his hand on Chase's back as he steered him toward the door. "No law that says you have to stay, but once you meet her, I'm thinking you'll want to, for sure."

Chase steeled himself for the force that was Beth in full matchmaking mode. Just as they went through the door, Carl said, "One thing. Try to act like you're okay with it? I know it kinda sucks going into this blind, but it means a lot to Beth. And anything that keeps her mind off what could go wrong in childbirth is good. I swear she's come up with every horror story there could be." Now he slapped Chase's back. "I owe you one. Big time."

"Fine."

Gil's was a big place, with tables and chairs scattered randomly, a long bar with mismatched chairs at different heights, a band platform in one corner and a large dance floor, worn and scarred by too many shoes to count over the years, in front of it.

Posters of action movies lined the walls beneath animal mounts, mostly deer, but also one bear with his front paws raised in attack mode and his mouth wide open, revealing a chipped tooth. The lighting consisted mostly of bulbs strung through mason jars and hanging from the ceiling. The stale smell of beer, from days or maybe even years past, clung to every corner.

For the most part, it looked like a moonshiner's version of a hunting lodge. Not that it mattered. People didn't come to Gil's for the décor. They came for the generous pours, nonstop conversation, live music, and bad dancing. You didn't have to know anyone when you went into Gil's, but you sure as hell were going to know a lot of someones by the time you left.

Chase saw Carl slide a small video camera from the pocket of his jacket and grip it in his hand.

"Ignore this thing," Carl said. "We're over there."

Carl led the way and Chase followed, squinting to see ahead. First person he saw was Beth, who rose from her seat with some difficulty to greet him, a smile on her face so bright and wide, she could have powered all of Gil's mason jar lights on her own. "Chase," she said, smothering him in a vanilla-scented hug. "Thank you for coming," she said in his ear. "You never know, you might have fun."

She and her husband must synch up their pep talks ahead of time, Chase decided. He turned to the other woman seated at the table with a smile that faded as soon as she pushed back her chair to stand.

Emma. The woman who stubbornly taken up residence in his brain, weaving through every single conscious and unconscious thought, ever since she'd shocked the hell out of him by showing up out of nowhere last night.

"Emma Zane, meet Chase Chapman," Beth said.

"Hi," Emma said. "Nice to meet you." She extended her hand. Even in the dim lighting, he could see a warning and a plea in her eyes. *Please play along.*

Fuck that. He didn't have to play along with her or anyone else. From the corner of his eye, Chase saw Carl zoom in for a close up of his wife and then move the camera toward the two she was introducing.

"Chase Chapman, meet Emma Zane," Beth continued, barely able to contain herself, she was so excited.

Every swear word Chase had ever learned was running through his mind, forming expletive-laden sentences. If anyone were to tap into his head, he'd be rated NA—as suitable for *No Audiences*. He was having trouble breathing.

"Chase?" Beth asked uncertainly. She rested a hand on her stomach, darting a look at her husband, who still had the camera on Chase, but was peeking out from around it, worry lining his face.

He couldn't do this to them. Not to Carl and Beth. Emma— He'd deal with her later.

He stuck his hand out to grip Emma's. Too hard, maybe. She made a little squeak, but kept smiling. "Nice to meet you," he said, teeth clenched.

"Great, great," breathed Beth. "Let's all sit down."

They did, with much scraping and bumping of chairs.

"Emma's into music. Just like you, Chase," Beth said.

"Is she now." He watched Emma take a long, slow drink of beer.

"She teaches it, in fact."

A teacher. Yeah, right. He tipped his head.

Emma took another slug of beer.

"Chase is a fabulous guitarist," Beth went on. "He plays with Carl's band."

"Really." Emma cleared her throat. "What kind of music?"

Carl peered out from behind the camera. "Country, mostly."

"My favorite," Emma said without taking her eyes off Chase.

Damn, but she looked good. She had on a sleeveless light-colored top that was short and loose, but managed to cling to her body. In places, it had jagged cutouts that looked sheer, revealing a black bra beneath. Her long, silver necklace had a pendant dangling from it that nestled between her breasts and when she stood up, he'd caught sight of tight jeans hugging her legs.

She'd done well in Nashville and it showed. So what did that say for him? All people did was keep fucking telling him to have fun. A band started up in the corner, He pounded down half the beer Carl had set in front of him.

His friend put down the camera. Then he motioned toward Emma. "She likes roller coasters."

Chase looked away from the what-the-hell-man question Carl was aiming at him. But then he saw Beth, who had a furrow between her brows. Her hand was rubbing her stomach.

Chase rounded the table. "So, let's dance," he said to Emma. He didn't wait for agreement, just took her hand and led her to the dance floor, making his way around several couples already swarming it. The band was playing some form of country rock heavy on drums and light on everything else. People at Gil's were an easy crowd, music-wise. They didn't ask for much, didn't get it, and didn't care. As long as there was plenty of beer.

Chase maneuvered Emma to the corner furthest from Beth and Carl and swung her into a two-step. She fell easily into it, laying her hand on his bicep and sending jolts of anticipation through him.

He looked past her, at a couple dressed in matching shirts, hoping they'd distract him from the warm, familiar curves of Emma's body as he rested his hand on the small of her back. Didn't work.

"Want to tell me what's going on?" he asked.

Emma started at the feel of his hand on her back but maintained her composure by keeping her posture rigid, by pretending it was somebody else's hand. Anyone else's. But it wasn't; it was Chase's hand. No one else had ever held her so gently and so fiercely all at the same time.

She did not want to tell him what was going on, but she supposed she owed him that.

"You wouldn't talk to me when I came all the way here to see you," she said, lifting her voice to be heard over the drummer. "And I wanted us to talk."

"So you found my friends and talked them into setting us up by pretending you don't know me, that we've never met."

"It wasn't like that," she said, before grudgingly adding, "Well, it was sort of like that. But it didn't start out that way." Whatever he was doing at that old place was working his muscles. His arm was pleasantly hard beneath her hand. She resisted the urge to let her fingers explore further.

"I told you there's nothing to talk about."

"We have unfinished business."

He pulled away, just far enough to look into her eyes with his own. The color had always made her think of lush, rolling fields, washed by the sun and fed by the rain. She'd never been able to look away when he locked her in with that gaze, any more than she could now.

"Listen to me. Nothing's changed," he said.

"You can say that again," she managed to say. Her heart pounded hard enough to be heard over the band's drummer. Nothing *had* changed. Chase was still the man who could practically make her come by looking at her, while turning her nipples hard and her knees shaky. She pressed her fingers harder into his arm now, to make sure she could stay upright.

Nothing had changed. At least for her.

His jaw worked as though he was thinking about saying something, but instead he spun her around in time with the music. By the time she faced him again, she wasn't sure she was still breathing.

His thick, dark hair looked as though it had been washed and left to dry on its own. Bits of it, the bits that had a wave at the ends, stood up, at odds with each other, a testament to the fact that he rarely gave it much thought. The little time he spent on anything but get-soap-and-water-clean gave him a careless look that enhanced his natural good looks more than any stylist could.

His nose was only semi-straight after being broken in a long-ago baseball game where his team had emerged the victor. His chin was strong and defined, a chin that had a stubborn set to it, but one that wouldn't back down from a challenge, one that wouldn't let you down.

No wonder she found Jason Jeffries wanting.

"Hey, you two." They stopped dancing and Carl appeared with his camera held high. "How about you lean in, nice and close?"

Hell, yes, Emma wanted to say, but when she looked up at Chase, a storm appeared to be rolling across his face. She hesitated. She wanted to grab him, pull him toward her and tell him how much she'd gone through to be here, to make it right with him again. But she didn't do any of that. Instead, she stared at the dark grey t-shirt stretched across his chest and wished she'd never gone to see Madame Claire. She must look dorky and pathetic standing here, like the worst kind of awkward loser—

He suddenly pulled her close to him, and she felt the brush of his whiskers and warmth of his skin against her cheek as he said, "Sure," to Carl.

Emma might be the only one who could tell that his jaw was clenched as he said it.

For her part, she was pretty sure she looked as startled, aroused, and confused as she felt, but Carl seemed satisfied. After a minute or so of filming, accompanied by his good-natured narration about the "happy couple," he moved off, presumably to bring Beth the good news that her matchmaking appeared to have worked.

Chase and Emma, on the other hand, didn't move, even as couples danced around them. She wasn't going to be the first to pull away and apparently, neither was he. She could swear she heard his heart beating now, though it could have been hers, since it seemed to have gone into overdrive.

He turned ever so slightly until they were opposite each other, their faces inches apart. His breath was warm on her face. His brows and his jaw muscles worked. Then he reached up to brush her hair back in a gesture so familiar and tender, it sent memories flooding back in a rush.

He was going to kiss her. Right here on the dance floor. She'd missed his kisses, so, so much. More than anything. Well, *almost* anything. Heat flooded her. Thank God she had on her prettiest, laciest, most minimal underwear. Right now, she wouldn't care if he took here on the dance floor of Gil's. Those other people, whose presence she could barely acknowledge, could find their way home and leave her and Chase alone.

Now, *now,* she silently screamed at him. Oh to hell with waiting. She closed the distance between them for their mouths to meet.

He drew back.

Emma dropped her arms and stared at the floor, embarrassed. He didn't even want to kiss her, this man who had once sworn he couldn't live without her. She folded her arms across her chest and held herself tight.

"What happened?"

What happened? I let myself think you still had feelings for me when I should have known *better.* Emma wished she were back in the relative safety of her classroom, instead of here with Chase, sinking like a deflated balloon to the floor.

"Your hair. What happened?"

It took a few seconds for Emma's brain to clear. "Oh." She'd worked so hard to cover it, she'd forgotten about Madame Claire's slip of the scissors. "It was an accident." She dared a glance up at him.

"An accident." He looked as though he was trying not to laugh. "Did you do it?"

"Of course not." She was still confused, but also beginning to feel irritated. "The hair stylist did." So what. A little chunk of her bangs had gone missing. Wasn't nearly as big a deal as him rebuffing a kiss from her. Wait…had he?

A couple with matching shirts bumped into them, but continued merrily on.

"That's some hair stylist."

Emma moved beyond irritated to a rolling boil that began somewhere in her thwarted lower regions and shot upward. She jammed her hands on her hips. "Unlike you, *I* don't hold a grudge." Her voice shook. "Anyone can make a mistake."

The thundercloud she'd seen earlier appeared to be rolling back through. "Sure. Unless it wasn't a mistake."

"Like she *planned* on doing it."

"Could be. You never know what someone is capable of."

"A mistake, Chase. Do you get that? Sometimes people make mistakes. Because they're human."

"But they only say it was a mistake when they get caught." He narrowed his eyes.

Emma had never stamped her foot in her life, but she did it now. Unfortunately, it was timed with the drummer's downbeat, so it didn't have the sound effect she was after. But it still felt good. Or childish. "You just refused to see why I did it, why I had to. Because of your damn pride."

He leaned in closer, until their noses nearly touched. "Trust me. Nothing got in the way of me seeing why you did it."

Around them, people continued to dance, sing, shout to their friends. As if life was carrying on fine, while Emma's heart broke. A second time.

"I didn't mean for it to look like I didn't believe in you. In our partnership. I *did*." Her breath caught on the last word.

"Not when it counted."

She shook her head. "Not true. If you'd give me a chance, you'd see that."

"I don't go down the same road twice."

"But what if it takes a different turn the next time?" It could happen. She should know.

Slowly, carefully, her heart in her throat, she raised her hands to lay them on either side of his face, gently caressing the contours of his jaw and brushing her fingers across his lips. She felt his sharp intake of breath and saw his eyes began to close, then fly open again.

The Emma Zane she'd always been would never take matters into her own hands, would never make the first move to seduce a man who was angry with her and, worse than that, unable to forget she'd once hurt him.

But that Emma Zane was still in Seattle, frustrated, bitter, and scared to death. *This* Emma Zane was someone different. Someone who was done looking back and ready to take what she wanted. A person both Emmas might like a lot.

Emma put her lips on Chase's, lightly at first and then hard and hungry, daring him to make her stop. She felt him respond, his chest muscles clenching, his arms folding around her, pulling her close.

But neither old nor new Emma Zane could have predicted what happened next.

CHAPTER THIRTEEN

Chase gripped Emma's upper arms and pushed back. She stared at him, breathing hard. Then he pulled her in again, harder, and her breath left her yet again as his mouth closed over hers. It was so right and had been so long…

From somewhere far away, she heard a voice knifing at the edges of her consciousness. It sounded familiar. Amplified. Alarming. She became aware of a sense of space around the two of them that hadn't been there before. She opened her eyes. People were moving away, spreading into the corners of the dance floor. Smiling people.

Chase now, too, seemed to be aware of it. He drew back, looking around them. From the stage, a female voice was saying something about love stories. In an odd accent.

Noooooo. Emma turned toward the band's corner. There, with a guitar strapped around her and a red-and-white checked dress straight out of the fifties, was Madame Claire, silver hair and all. "Is it not a love song we need?" she asked the Gil's patrons. When they looked at each other, murmuring questions, she demanded, "Is it *not*?"

Lots of answering nods then and rumbles of assent, with hands risen to clap but not quite achieving it. Confused and half drunk as the Gil's crowd might be, they were polite.

Chase looked at Emma, at the stage, and back at Emma, questions in his eyes.

"These two people," Madame Claire gestured at Chase and Emma, "they are perfect for the other."

Emma's heart sank. This could not be going anywhere good.

"Who is that?" Chase asked.

"My hair stylist."

"Your *what*?"

And then Madame Claire began singing "Stand by Your Man," her voice way too high. *Sometimes hard it is to be a woe-men*, she warbled. Emma cringed.

The band dutifully took up the appropriate musical accompaniment, a good thing since Madame Claire's strum of the guitar had nothing to do with the melody.

Emma wanted to shake her, pull her off the stage and demand to know what she thought she was doing, but at the same time, she couldn't help feeling grateful that the *woe-man* was trying so hard to help. And doing such a bang-up bad job of it.

People continued to stare at her and Chase, smiles wreathing their faces, even as they looked in confusion at Madame Claire, who dreamily sang, *But if it is you love him, it is you'll forgive him* with as much conviction as if she were a semi-southern Yoda, onstage at the Ryman. In a red-and-white-checked dress and leopard-print heels.

"Seriously. Your hair stylist thinks this is a love song."

"You've seen my bangs." She stopped herself just short of adding, *and my do-over.*

"Right."

Madame Claire finished her song and took an awkward bow to the smatterings of applause. She had just stepped back to the microphone when the band took over, pounding out the opening of a Blake Shelton song. Madame Claire valiantly joined in with her one-note strum as someone with the band discreetly moved the mic away from her.

People surged back onto the dance floor. Chase turned to Emma and gave her a smile that sent anticipation shivering up her spine. "What the hell. Let's dance," he said.

It wasn't the most romantic invitation she'd ever heard, but this was Chase. And he'd just taken a big step, possibly toward forgiving her.

He spun her as lightly and effortlessly as he once had and she fell into the familiar rhythm of dancing in his arms. When the song finished, she was breathless, and it wasn't from the physical exertion. *He might still love me, at least he doesn't hate me, he might still love me,* kept running through her mind until she was sure the words were flashing across her face like a giant billboard.

For once, just once, she would like to be someone who could hide her feelings. The kind of woman who could keep people guessing until she was ready to reveal.

But she wasn't. She was read-me-like-a-book Emma. Want to know something? *Just look at my face.*

The band finished the song and the people on the floor stopped long enough to applaud. On the stage, Madame Claire bobbed up and down in a bow, her silver hair flashing in the lights. Then she ducked between the bass guitarist and drummer to exit the stage as the band began to strike up the notes for a slow song.

The lead guitarist, his dark tangled hair as sad as his baggy clothing, stepped up to the microphone with the faraway expression of a vocalist determined to take them all on an emotional journey. Emma saw a flash of red and white checks from the corner of her eye and grabbed Chase's hand. "Over here."

She led him away from the center of the crowd, maneuvering behind the matching-shirt couple so she could use them as a shield to hide from Madame Claire. There had already been enough interference from Carl and Beth; she didn't need one more person piling on to ensure the "blind date" was going well. At this rate, Emma would consider herself very lucky if Madame Claire didn't next show up as the bar's bouncer.

Emma wrapped her arms around Chase's neck and began moving her hips along with the music and the vocalist's soulful, if slightly off-tune, rendition of the lyrics. After a hesitation, Chase responded, bringing his own arms around Emma, his hands holding her lightly as he too began to sway.

She inhaled his blend of soap, sawdust, and shave cream, thinking that she wanted to continue like this forever, until he could see how much she'd missed him, how big the hole in her heart had become after he'd left. Gently, softly, she pushed her fingers into his shoulders, urging him closer.

He bent his head, bringing his cheek close enough to hers that she could feel the warmth coming from his skin. Her knees wibbled and wobbled, threatening to give way. Much more of this and she'd have an orgasm right here on the dance floor. She could only hope her ecstatic scream would be timed with the vocalist's high notes.

She was working up her nerve to whisper an invitation in his ear that involved the backseat of his truck when the music stopped. Chase took a step back, raising his hands to clap for the band.

Emma pressed her own hands to her warm, damp cheeks, dropping her chin to let her hair cover them as voices raised and dropped around her in laughter, drunken conversation, blatant flirtation. At the very least, Madame Claire could have given her an instruction manual for this do-over. At this point, she didn't know if she was old Emma, new Emma or any Emma at all.

She raised her head to venture a glance at Chase, but her attention was instead caught by a woman crossing the floor toward the band platform. She got close, circled back, and tried it again, shaking her wrists until they looked like they belonged to a rag doll.

It was Chrissy, from the salon. Working up her courage. She looked stricken with terror and, as she was circling back further than she was moving ahead, she was going to reach the exit sooner than the band platform.

"Oh, no," Emma breathed. "She can't leave. Not after she's made it this far."

Chase followed her gaze. "I know her."

"Me, too. Chrissy!" Emma called, giving a thumbs-up when the other woman turned in her direction. Chrissy pulled to an abrupt stop, her eyes wide.

"How long have you been here that you know people?" Chase asked.

"It just happens." Then she remembered what Chrissy had said about Chase and looked the other woman over with a sharper eye.

Gone was the nondescript outfit Chrissy had worn at the salon. She now had on form-fitting mint ankle jeans and a low-cut striped t-shirt. On her feet, she wore deep purple pumps that added several inches of height to her tiny frame. And she'd pulled her dark hair into a side pony that accentuated her high cheekbones and red lips.

Emma stole a glance at Chase, who was watching Chrissy. "She looks different," he observed.

No shit. "Beth is looking for you." She grasped his upper arm, steering him toward the table. "I'll be there in a minute."

"Chase!" Beth waved at him.

Chrissy stood rooted to her spot near the edge of the dance floor, one foot ahead of the other. Emma recognized the ready-to-flee position; she'd used it many times herself. She approached carefully, palms up.

When she reached the woman, she grasped her hand. "You're here. And you look great."

Chrissy shook her head. "I don't know what made me think I could do this. I'm leaving."

"No, you're not."

The other woman's expression flitted between scared and exasperated. "I'm going home. Why do you care?"

"Because I've been there. And I'm *not* letting you make the same mistake I did." The words were out before Emma could think about them. She dropped Chrissy's hand as though it were a hot coal, taken aback.

Chrissy looked over her shoulder at the band and then back at Emma. "Do you know what the worst thing would be? If they got quiet. And then polite, because they didn't want to hurt my feelings. I—I couldn't take that." She lifted her eyes.

"Bullshit," Emma shot back. Who *was* she? "The worst would be if you don't get up there and try tonight and then you go home and wonder what it would have been like. Because you couldn't get yourself on that stage."

Enough doubt flickered through Chrissy's eyes that Emma seized on the opening. "What's more horrible," she asked. "Wondering if you would have been a failure or knowing that you were because you didn't show up to try?"

"I…I…" Chrissy's arms flailed.

"Come on." Emma took her arm. "You want to do this; you know you do." She led the Chrissy toward the band, which was just finishing its number. The bass guitarist continued a few notes past the end and then looked at his bandmates in apology.

Emma pulled a protesting Chrissy behind her, up the few steps to the black platform that constituted the stage. With a nod at the band, she gestured toward the microphone and mouthed, "May I?"

The drummer shrugged and crossed his arms, while the bass guitarist swept a hand toward the mic.

"Could I have your attention?" Emma said. Those on the dance floor and those seated at tables turned to look at her. She purposely directed her gaze away from the Chase, Beth, and Carl table. Then she took a deep breath and put on her best teacher voice. "This young woman has never sung in public before, but she's always wanted to. I'm sure you and the band will be gracious enough to let her sing…" She stopped, leaned over and whispered to Chrissy, "What song?"

The terrified woman choked out the name of another Blake Shelton tune. Emma turned back to the band and gave it to them. They nodded.

"Please welcome Chrissy…uh…" She didn't know her last name. "*Chrissy*."

Obligatory applause. With a quiet, "Show 'em what you've got," Emma crossed the stage.

Chrissy took a step forward and gripped the microphone as a drowning woman would a life jacket. The band began to play. When it was time for her to sing, Chrissy opened her mouth and closed it again, looking down.

The band members looked at each other, stopped, and then started the song again. Emma hissed from the side of the stage, "This is your chance, shampoo girl!"

That seemed to snap Chrissy out of her haze. She began to sing, in a voice that started out high, shaky, and sweet. Around her, the crowd called encouragement and threw in a few appreciative whistles. Chrissy closed her eyes and her voice became stronger.

More applause from the crowd.

Midway through the song, her confidence growing, Chrissy began to move her hips to the music and some of the sugar spilled from her voice, replaced by something spicier.

More whistles as the first song came to a close. The audience clapped in appreciation as Chrissy, her cheeks flushed in an irritatingly adorable Taylor Swift sort of way, bowed, the microphone still in one hand.

Emma climbed down from the platform, clapping until her palms stung.

She heard a voice behind her. "Didn't know she could sing," Chase said.

The band struck up another song and a blushing Chrissy began high-stepping across the stage in her purple heels. Emma grabbed Chase's hand. "Let's dance."

"I don't remember you being this bossy," he grumbled.

"It's new. I've been practicing." Emma glanced back at the stage. Wait a minute. Was Chrissy looking at Chase? She was. She was singing directly to Chase while rocking her hips.

No problem. Really, no problem. Emma could be happy for Chrissy without falling prey to jealousy. Sure, she could. Probably. If only her sense of reason would have a talk with her emotions, but they usually attended separate parties, so it wasn't likely that was happening soon.

She took a deep breath, wondering how to get back to that invitation she'd been about to whisper in Chase's ear, but she suddenly wasn't as sure he'd accept. Why did life have to be so *complicated?* "Have you forgiven me yet?"

"Are you kidding?" His voice was rough.

Her heart lifted. She might not have to report Madame Claire to the psychic governing board, or whatever body policed her activities, after all. And she and Chase could finally be together—

"No," he said.

Emma stopped dancing. "What do you mean, no?"

"It's not that easy."

She took his hand, pulling him to an empty spot across the room, away from the speakers. "It sure as hell is. You say, 'Oh I'm sorry, I had it all wrong, I shouldn't have been such a jerk, I didn't realize what you were trying to do for us.' Then I say, that's okay, because you *didn't* know what I was trying to do and I should have been better about explaining it, and really you were kind of a jerk, but I say, let's start all over and forget about what happened then. Because there's only *now* and *then* doesn't really matter. Then I say, 'right?' And you say, 'right.'" She stopped to take a breath, her shoulders heaving.

One corner of his mouth lifted. "You've got it all planned out."

"Not really."

He tipped his head.

"Okay, sort of."

"So what happens next? That is, if this whole conversation actually happens and it isn't just in your head. Which is the only place it is right now. Just so we're clear on that."

She gave up the battle and let her smile slide across her face, running a light finger along his arm. "Well, then we—"

"How's it going?" Beth appeared at Emma's side.

Emma's shriek was small, but mighty. "Sorry," she choked out. "You startled me."

At Chase's side, Carl focused the video camera. "Having a good time, kids?"

"Sure," Chase answered. "Good time."

"Great!" Beth sounded pleased. "Time for my promo." Carl turned the camera on her and she began to speak into it.

Beth gave the camera a knowing, solemn nod. "There *is* someone just for you. If you would like your own Match Made in Maven, call me at the number below." She pointed down, presumably toward a phone number. "I'll find your happy ever after."

Beth scooped her and Chase into view of the camera. "You can be as happy as these two. All you have to do is call me. Right now."

"And...cut!" Carl said. He beamed at his wife. "Great job, honey."

Beth gave Emma and Chase each a side hug and then released them. She put her hand on her stomach. "We'd better get going, Carl. This kid and all of this matchmaking have worn me out."

Carl put an arm around his wife and began leading her toward the exit, but not before she'd turned back to give Emma and Chase a happy wave.

Someone else was heading toward them, Emma saw. A flushed, but happy Chrissy, her thumbs hooked into the belt loops of her skintight jeans and her gaze zeroed in on the back of Chase's head. He didn't see her, which meant he also didn't see the silver-haired country singer-slash-hair stylist–slash-psychic hip-check her out of the way.

Chrissy stumbled to one side on her purple shoes while Madame Claire gravely nodded at Emma.

"Let's dance," Emma said to Chase, grabbing his hand to lead him away.

"Quit telling me what to do," he said as she wrapped her arms around his neck and began swaying in time to the music.

"Sorry. But you might want to get used to it."

His arms circled her waist. Firm, strong, in control. "Why? You sticking around?"

Her jeans pressed against his and she felt his penis through the fabric, rigid and ready. She remembered that penis all too well and the places it had taken her, places she'd not gone since They began moving their hips as one as her breasts pressed into his warm, muscular chest and her heartbeat picked up speed. "I don't know. This place isn't so bad," she said softly.

"It isn't Nashville." His voice had turned husky; his eyes were half closed.

From the corner of her eye, she saw that Chrissy had regained her balance and was pushing the hair that had escaped her side pony from her eyes. She had a determined look in her eyes, but once again, was thwarted by Madame Claire who grabbed her elbow and steered her back in the direction of the stage.

Emma was pretty sure she should have laughed, or at least cared, but right now, all she could think of was the way Chase's breath appeared to be more labored, of the aroused state of her own body, where all rational thought seemed to be fleeing for its life while pure, aching physical desire took over. She caressed Chase's warm, damp neck with her fingers. God help her, she wanted nothing but to see the other side of Gil's door right now.

The music stopped. Chase and Emma didn't.

Emma was vaguely conscious of the band beginning to play, somewhere in the background. She was more conscious of Chase guiding her toward the exit. She tried not to get too ahead of herself with anticipation. Tonight, everything would be repaired between them. Better than it had ever been. She lifted her chin, letting her hair fall back and reveling in the feelings that had been bottled up for far too long.

Just wait until Chase Chapman slipped under the covers with the new Emma Zane. Hell, maybe the new Emma Zane didn't need a bed. She'd find someplace a lot more adventurous.

She imagined Chase's eyes growing wide at where that might be and *who* the new Emma might be and couldn't help herself as a sound of pure joy slipped from her lips.

Then Chase stiffened and stopped moving. With effort, Emma pulled herself out of the haze of drowsy arousal enough to wonder if something was wrong.

He dropped his hands from her body and reached up to loosen her hold on him. Then he took a step back. Emma fought her way back to the surface and refocused her eyes. His had turned cold.

The band was playing. Chrissy was singing again, the words frighteningly familiar.

It all starts with a wish
Carries on with a kiss
And the one you've longed for
Is making your heart soar
Tying it up with a twist

Why? Of all the songs, why *this* one? Why now? Emma clutched a fistful of Chase's t-shirt, holding on.

When you wish some,

Hope some,
Try some
Die some…

Chase grasped her hand, pulling it away. "I can't do this."

"It's a song, that's all," she pleaded. "It's in the past."

Pain contorted his face, but was quickly replaced by determination. "My past. Your future." He shook her off and began walking away.

"Chase," she pleaded with his back.

No response. He disappeared through the door.

And out of her life.

CHAPTER FOURTEEN

After the noise and chaos of Gil's, the quiet of The Earl Walker hotel should have been a relief, but instead, it gave Emma's mind too much room to think, relive, second-guess. She opened the door to her room and headed straight for the four-poster bed and its fluffy white bedding, landing with a plop in the center of it, her fist hitting a pillow that had done nothing to deserve it.

If only she'd not decided to go to a hair salon. *If only* she'd left well enough alone with Chrissy and not encouraged to try her luck at singing. *If only* "Wishsome" had never played at Gil's. *If only*...Emma had not gone to a psychic who had dangled the tantalizing idea of regaining a love she'd lost, which would only end up staying lost.

The *if only* game never worked out well.

Emma tried clearing her mind with math problems, by reading the newspaper that had been pushed under the door, by doing the crossword in the paper, and by lying on her back and conjuring up images of every vacation destination she'd ever wanted to travel to, but never had.

After an hour or so had passed, she'd solved as many math problems as she could think of, read newspaper articles on the adventures of the Coupons and Conversation Club, the local kid appointed to West Point and the one who had helped shelter animals as a part of her Girl Scout project, gained summer gardening tips, and become up to date on everything happening at the senior center. Which wasn't a whole lot, other than the upcoming Just Say No to Bunions seminar.

Still the evening with Chase knotted her stomach, refusing to leave.

She went over her familiar list of someday vacation spots, but became confused when it felt as though she might have been to some of them, with the memory hovering just out of her reach. Belize...Jamaica...an overwater bungalow in Bora Bora. She heard the lapping of water beneath the floorboards, basked in the warmth of sun on her face, squinted at the vivid contrasts of blues, greens and whites. Had she been there? Why couldn't she remember?

Chase lingered at the beginning and end of every thought and fought his way into the middle, offering answers to the math problems, adding to the coupon conversation, claiming he would never have bunions, settling in on a chaise lounge at the overwater bungalow.

Weighing so heavy on her heart that she thought it must have sunk to somewhere around her feet by now.

Emma pushed herself off the bed and padded into the white bathroom. She turned on the old-fashioned faucet and began running a lukewarm bath, in deference to the still-warm night breeze that ruffled the curtains at the windows.

Soaking in a tub. The perfect antidote to a too-active mind.

She peeled off her clothing, left it in a heap on the tile floor, and stepped into the water. Then she lay back against the cool porcelain, letting the ends of her hair float in the water. She put her feet up on the side of the tub and marveled at how good her toes looked with their flawless pedicure.

She trailed her fingers through the water, back and forth, trying to recreate the sounds she might hear in that overwater bungalow. *Damn.* If new Emma had ever been there, old Emma really, really wanted to remember. It seemed only fair.

A tear rolled from the corner of one eye and then the next. *I didn't even realize how much I loved him.*

According to the local paper, the seniors in town were hosting a pig roast, with an actual spit and everything. It would be overseen by an eighty-eight-year-old recognized barbecue master—how did a person even achieve that designation? She hoped he didn't get too close to the fire. His reflexes might have slowed.

I wonder what Chase is thinking right now; I hope it's not that he made a narrow escape. Or maybe he's not thinking at all. He's sound asleep. I'm the only one in the whole town who can't sleep, can't shut off the late-night program running in my head.

The tears became bigger, the rolls down her cheeks faster, until they formed continuous streams that fell from her chin onto her chest.

The Coupon and Conversation Club named a Savings Star each month. Emma imagined a fierce competition among the club members that led to back alley coupon dealing. A mom in leather, under the cover of night, with a baggie of prized $5-off coupons stuffed into a secret pocket of her purse.

How can he not be thinking of me, wondering about me, beating himself up for being so stupid over one song? Even if it had been the song they had spent the most time on together, the one they couldn't ever finish.

But she'd apparently finished it with Jason. That had to have wounded Chase and she was sorry, so sorry about it. She wished she knew how it had happened. By all appearances, that new Emma could be a real bitch sometimes.

The tears were now running down her boobs and launching into the bath water that was turning cooler by the second. And saltier.

Beside her on the floor, her cell phone rang. She grabbed it quick, before looking at caller ID. It could only be one person. *Chase.*

She sniffed big and swiped at the tears on her cheek before clicking the green icon to answer. "Hello?"

"*Finally* you pick up. I know it's late, but I've been going crazy worrying about you. And that assistant of yours, what's her name, Teri or something, won't talk."

Not Chase. Emma's mind raced, trying to place the voice.

"Emma? You there?"

"Yes."

"I'm hoping you weren't answering because you were finishing those lyrics." It was expressed as a demand, not a hope.

Jason. She squeezed her eyes shut tight. "I'm working on it," she lied. "And leave my assistant alone. She doesn't have anything to do with it."

"When will they be done?"

"Soon, Jason," she whispered. "Soon."

She opened her eyes and clicked the phone off while he was still talking or, more accurately, ranting. She would deal with Jason Jeffries later. Or not at all.

Emma shivered. The water had gone from cool to cold. *Is he thinking about me?*

A voice rose from deep within her to shout, *There's only one fucking way to find out. Grow up, get your clothes on and get the hell out of here.*

Whether it was new Emma, old Emma, or some Emma in between who yelled, she obeyed, straightening immediately and kicking the old-fashioned stopper from the drain to let the water out.

A few minutes later, she'd dried off, run a comb through the wet ends of her hair and thrown on a pair of jeans and a low-cut t-shirt. She slid sandals onto her feet, grabbed her purse and her car keys, and was out the door of the room before she had time to think about where she was going.

Because if she had stopped to think about where she was going, she might have turned the car back toward Nashville instead of heading for Chase Chapman's farmhouse.

***

Pounding. His head was pounding. Chase swum from the depths of his uneasy, alcohol-fueled sleep, thinking he'd better get some aspirin or he'd regret it in the morning, which might be arriving way too soon.

Then he realized the pounding was coming from the front door and his head was only going along for the ride.

Lila barked an alarm.

Who the fuck was pounding on his door in the middle of the night? It'd better be a damn emergency.

He pulled on the closest pair of jeans and stumbled, shirtless and barefoot, to the door. "Ouch! Shit." He stepped on something and pulled his foot up, limping the rest of the way. He fumbled and found the switch for the lamp. The pounding continued. "Hold *on*." He threw open the door, letting it hit and bounce back from the wall.

In front of him stood Emma, her fist still in the air. Her eyes were as wild and as angry as his probably were and her cheeks were bright pink. The ends of her hair were wet and sticking to the white t-shirt stretched across her chest. Behind her, male crickets chirped their mating call into the summer night.

He became aware of his breathing, short and sharp. Of the floorboard pressing into the bare soles of his feet. Of her proximity. Of his dick, traitorously standing at attention and pulling his jeans tight.

The crickets apparently weren't the only ones looking to get laid.

"What are you doing here?" he asked a lot more calmly than he felt.

"Coming inside."

He thought about making a smart-ass remark, but in the end, he just stepped aside and let her pass. He guided the door closed with a care he hadn't taken when he'd jerked it open. *Don't look at her boobs; don't think about the way her ass would feel in your hands.* "Coffee?" he asked her forehead.

"I don't want coffee."

"Fine. Have a seat." He sprawled onto one of the battered leather couches and pulled Lila close when she jumped up beside him. If he positioned the dog right, Emma would never have to know how the mere sight of her, the slightest hint of her scent, turned him on. All this time and he still had it bad for her. *You're fucking pitiful, Chapman.*

The leather of the couch opposite him sighed as she sat down. She clasped her hands in front of her until the knuckles turned white.

He turned his attention to the dog, scratching softly behind Lila's ears. And waited for Emma to speak, even as a torrent of things he might, but wouldn't, say rushed through his head, on a virtual freeway, exceeding the speed limit. Whoosh. There went...*you're even more beautiful as a woman than you were as a teenager.* Zip. Off flew...*get out of my house.* Screech. Past the exit ramp went...*never leave me.*

With an abrupt shove off the leather, he stood. "I don't care if you want coffee. I do."

"Then I'll have some, too."

The quiet control in her voice signaled danger to him. He'd seen what was in her eyes and it wasn't quiet. Or controlled. Chase opened and closed cupboards in the kitchen more loudly than he needed to and turned the water on with a decisive yank. Before long, the coffeepot was rumbling to life, filling the small kitchen with its aroma.

Chase pushed the heels of his hands into the countertop and hung his head, trying to think what to do next. The only thing he could come up with was that he had no idea. He didn't want to talk. He didn't *not* want to talk.

Basically, he was screwed either way.

"Where are the cups?"

Startled, Chase brought his head up too fast and swayed on his feet. Emma put a hand out, catching his arm. He regained his balance and walked out of her grasp, toward the cupboard that held an assortment of ancient mugs. The one he chose for Emma read, *Maven Hardware. More nuts than bolts. Since 1965.* The one he grabbed for himself had a faded drawing of a John Deere tractor.

He held the Maven Hardware mug out to her and they waited in silence until the coffeepot beeped to signal it was done. They reached for it at the same time, their fingers brushing. Chase looked at Emma; she looked at Chase and pulled her hand away. "You go ahead," she said.

He lifted the coffee and waited until she held out her mug, then poured the hot liquid into it, careful not to spill. He filled his own mug and gestured toward the living room.

It was all so formal and restrained, he thought something inside him might break out yelling, just to hear a sound. But nothing did, so he followed Emma in to the other room and sat back down on the sofa, where Lila looked up at him with a puzzled expression. He patted her and bits of fur flew upward, spiraling and falling in the light of the lamp.

"You left," Emma said, breaking the silence. Her voice broke on the last word. She looked away.

He stared down at the mug of coffee in his hands. "Look, I…" He couldn't think of what else to say. Nothing seemed right. He wasn't good at this shit. "I had to."

"Things were going great. We were having fun. Didn't it feel like that to you?"

"I was going along with it for Beth. I told you that." He looked up at the ceiling. "And then—I forgot for a while."

"Forgot." She wrapped her arms tighter around herself, her eyes wide.

"How it was between us. When you left me."

"When *I* left."

What the hell? He leaned forward, knees spread, hands clasped between them. "Yes. When *you* left."

"Oh." She looked confused. "I thought you kicked me out."

"Don't rewrite history," he warned. "I told you to give Jeffries back his money or leave."

"We had rent due," she said slowly, as if only remembering it only now. "We needed the money. I couldn't give it back." Her voice lifted, leaving the words dangling like a question.

What was she doing, claiming amnesia? That wasn't gonna fly. "I told you I'd get the rent money," he shot.

She shook her head. "Your pride. That's all it was ever about. You had to be the one to pay the rent."

He pulled his mouth tight. His *pride*. She didn't get it; she never had.

"You didn't want the money because it came from Jason Jeffries."

His eyes met hers. "Nothing about that time matters anymore." He silently congratulated himself on finally acquiring the ability to lie. If she bought it.

She didn't.

"If it didn't matter anymore, you wouldn't have walked out tonight."

He sat back hard, raking a hand through his hair. "What matters is that you didn't tell me anything, Emma. I had to hear it from that asshole while I was working the bar. He comes in, orders a drink and starts telling me all about this sweet deal he's made with a songwriter." His fist pounded his thigh as he remembered. Lila moved to the other end of the sofa. "Talking all about how her lyrics were the best he'd ever heard and they were going to make a name for themselves."

"Chase—"

He wasn't stopping now. "I was only half listening. Everybody in Nashville's got some story like that. Then he said your name. Emma Zane. Remember it, he said. We're going to be big." He pushed through the memory, causing his voice to rasp against his throat like a million razor-sharp blades. "She's already done lyrics for two songs. You can't even fucking believe how good they are." He stood and began pacing. His voice was coming faster, his breath more ragged. "Then he said, she's gonna cut the guy she's been working with loose and it's gonna be me and her, the next big songwriting team."

Her face crumpled. "That can't be right."

"You think I didn't hear him right? I remember every word."

"He made it up. I never would have left you for him."

He thrust his chin in her direction. "But you did."

"I'm sorry. Really, really sorry." She touched a finger to her lips and held it there, as if afraid of what she might say next.

Or maybe what he would say. Yeah, she *should* be afraid of that.
Now that he'd gotten started, he might just keep going. "We were
close on 'Wishsome.' That song was ours. Only ours."

She moved her hand from her mouth. "I felt the same way."

"You couldn't have. You sold it to Jeffries."

"Only…afterward. After we broke up."

"And you won a CMA award for it. Good on you."

Emma stood, crossing the room to him, standing inches away.
"That didn't matter. I mean, sure, it's great to win an award, but
when you weren't there, it wasn't the same. Wasn't real. I couldn't
believe it when I found out Jason wrote the melody."

What the—? He narrowed his eyes, staring at her. "What do you
mean, you found out? You're not making any sense."

"It doesn't make sense that we left things the way we did. I want
another chance, Chase. Everybody makes mistakes and what Jason
told you was a lie. I wasn't planning on teaming up with him. I only
sold him—" She stopped, searching left and right with her eyes.
"Sold him lyrics for a couple of songs so I could get some money for
us. Songs I didn't care about. I didn't think it would matter to you. If
I'd known it would mean I'd lose you, I never would have done it,"
she pleaded.

He wanted so much to believe her. Her eyes, which had always
reminded him of the sparkling, pure blue water of the deep ocean,
were troubled and filled with tears. She swiped at them with the back
of her hand.

Her hair, which earlier in the night had curled around her
shoulders, so shiny it almost glowed, now looked as though the ends
had been run through a blender. The chunk out of her bangs was
sticking straight up. She had a streak of makeup under one eye. Her
shoes didn't match. And part of her bra was showing above the low
dip of her t-shirt.

The drive-him-insane-bad-ass-sexy part of it was that she didn't
care. Most women would later yell that he should have told them,
that they couldn't be seen this way.

Emma had never been like that. They'd been caught in a
rainstorm once and her hair, her makeup, and her clothes were
soaked and ruined. She'd looked in the mirror when they got home
and laughed so hard, she'd doubled over. They'd taken a photo of

themselves, just so they could pull it out from time to time and laugh all over again.

He still had it, slid into the pages of a book next to his bed. Not that he'd ever tell her that.

Yeah, he wanted to believe her something awful. His dick was signaling its willingness to, if not believe her, take her now. The small, feminine body in front of him, with its hard and soft curves, firm ass and perfect rounded boobs was calling him in the worst way. Until he ached with wanting her, like it used to be.

His mind kept getting in the way, though. Telling him not to be stupid, to remember this was Emma, who had hurt him in places he'd never before let anyone have access to. It wasn't going to happen again.

"Dammit, Chase, all I did was sell a couple of songs. I didn't cheat on you. I wouldn't do that." Her eyes turned wild again and her hand began flailing in distress. "But you can't forgive me, even when you know the reason I did it. Why? *Why?*"

"If you don't know, then you don't know me."

"I know you." She shook a finger at him now. "I love you." She caught herself, backtracked. "Loved you. Knew you better than anyone else."

Don't go there. *Don't.* Go there. He didn't want anybody loving him. Not anymore. It hurt too fucking much when it ended. Better to play, have fun. Leave. No ties.

"And you loved me," she said, her voice throaty, on the edge. "Maybe still do."

She'd gone there. Before he knew it, his arms were spread out to both sides and he was the one yelling, loud enough that Lila jumped from the couch and ran out of the room. "I did love you. We had something nobody else did. We were good—really, really good. You understand that?"

A mute nod.

"Then you threw it all away to write songs with somebody else, for money you thought I couldn't get for us. For *success* you thought I couldn't get for us."

"It wasn't like that!"

"The hell it wasn't. How did you expect me to feel, knowing you were sharing a part of your soul with somebody else? Somebody you thought could make it." Ow. Fuck; that one hurt.

"I believed in you!" she shouted right back. "Don't you ever tell me I didn't! You're just too stubborn to see things for what they are. We needed money."

"I may be stubborn," he said, recognizing the dangerous rumble his voice had taken on. A part of him wanted to stop right now, not keep going. Not say the thing he was about to. "But you're the one who can't trust anyone. You require proof ahead of time or at least a down payment. You don't—no, you *can't*—go on faith. Because your mother got burned and you're scared you'll turn into her. But guess what."

He saw her blink fast, saw her hold her breath.

"At least your mother can still feel something. Can still believe in somebody. You, on the other hand, turned that part of yourself off a long time ago."

Her mouth worked furiously as she looked everywhere but at him. Her nostrils flared and her chin quivered. Then she picked up her purse and walked out the door, closing it so softly behind her, it didn't make a sound.

He stood there for several minutes, not moving. At last, Lila padded back into the room, looking up at him with accusation in her eyes. It wasn't hard to read her thoughts. *Who's the asshole now?*

Just once, the dog could take his side.

CHAPTER FIFTEEN

Emma stumbled across the porch and away from the house, not caring where she was going or how she got there. Was he right? Was it true? Had she tried so hard to be the opposite of her mother that she'd turned into a person who could no longer genuinely care about or believe in someone?

It wasn't that hard to believe. She flashed back to the face of her assistant, who had looked terrified to make a mistake with her boss that night of the CMAs. To the mean things Emma had reportedly said about Etta Dorcas, who was a legend in the business.

She thought about Jason Jeffries, who had little on his mind but Jason Jeffries. Emma had apparently agreed to marry the self-obsessed chart climber. So she'd have something to tweet. What did that alone say about her?

Stars lent enough light for her to follow the dirt path toward her car. She scuffed her shoes in the dirt, hoping they were expensive. For some reason she couldn't pinpoint, that would make her feel better about ruining them.

Even her do-over request had been selfish, she decided with a hiccup that echoed over the sounds of the crickets. Chase had been a successful songwriter before she'd interfered; now he wasn't. And that was nothing short of a crime, given his talent.

To make things worse, she'd come back into his life assuming she could be a part of it again. Just like that. Because a crazy psychic had switched things up.

She didn't like herself much right now, so it was a sure bet no one else would or should, either.

The path ended. Emma looked up, realizing she hadn't reached the car. Instead, she'd followed a path somewhere else, to a small lake where the night stars glistened in the still, glass-like water. A long bench sat next to the edge.

Emma sank onto it gratefully, feeling the wooden slats beneath her. Around her, the air was heavy and slightly damp, but peaceful. The night critters went about their silent business, taking no notice of her.

123

She loved the water. Growing up in the northwest, lakes and the ocean had always been sanctuaries, places to contemplate her life, puzzle out problems, regroup and revive.

Sitting by the water was like no other place on earth—quiet, non-judgmental, calming. Given half a chance, it might bring order to the chaos in her mind.

She reached down to finger a pebble and threw it into the lake, where it plopped softly. *I'm sorry, Chase. For whoever I have been and still am.*

She gazed into the water for what seemed like forever, hearing only the occasional rustle in the grasses and disturbance in the lake. Fish, probably. She wondered if they ever slept. A yawn escaped her.

She should find the car, she thought. Instead, she lay down on the bench, her hands tucked beneath her head, and wished the ache in her stomach, the one that squeezed hard and climbed into her throat every time she thought of Chase, would subside.

Not that she didn't deserve it. She didn't deserve him; he was better off without her. Then *and* now. She deserved…what? Someone like Jason Jeffries, who put as little into a relationship as she did.

She took her cell out of her pocket and pulled up the number that had been calling her over and over. When Jason didn't answer, she breathed a sigh of relief and left him a message. "This is Emma. I'll be back tomorrow."

Then she closed her eyes and let the blackness envelop her.

The next thing she knew, her head was being gently lifted and placed on warm legs, clad in soft, worn denim. Sleepily, she stretched one leg and shifted it so that her hip bone could move from its position on the wooden bench.

A hand began stroking her hair. She opened her eyes, squinting at the brightening sky reflecting on the lake. "Hi," she said to Chase. She didn't have to look; she knew it was him. Knew the feel of his legs, his touch on her hair.

"Hi."

They fell silent. Something small and invisible skittered through the grass. "I meant to leave," Emma said at last.

"You didn't get far."

"I saw the lake."

He lifted a piece of her hair and smoothed it back, away from her face. "Remember that time we went to the San Juans?"

She let herself smile at the memory of the beautiful, pristine and remote Washington islands. "My mother never did find out I went away for the weekend with a boy. She still thinks I stayed the night at Anna's."

"I wanted to stay there forever, in Friday Harbor, just you and me. Never wanted to go back to the real world. I was hoping all the ferries would break down at the same time and we'd have no way to get home."

She braved a glance up. There was a faraway look in his eyes. "Me, too," she whispered.

After a minute, he spoke again, his voice rough, husky with emotion. "I know I'm hard-headed. I know my pride gets in the way. But that wasn't it."

She turned until the back of her head was lying in his lap and watched as his jaw worked. It took a while for him to speak again, but at last, he did. "If you couldn't believe in me, I figured—I couldn't believe in me."

"That's why you're not writing."

He choked out a half laugh and lifted one shoulder. "Hey, we always knew you were the talented one."

She took hold of his chin with her fingers, making him look at her. "I never doubted you." She pulled him closer, wanting to be sure he understood. "But some things, the things you learn in childhood, they don't leave. It was making me crazy living like that, with no security. No money in the bank."

"I should never have talked you into coming to Nashville with me. You would have been fine staying in Seattle."

"Oh no. I wouldn't have," she rushed to say.

"Right. I shouldn't have said that. You've done well." He hesitated and the stark honesty in his eyes caused her to catch her breath. "I'm proud of you."

She released her hold on him, letting her hand drop back down. "You can't give it up, Chase."

He looked away.

"Music is a part of you."

"Then someday I'll go back to it."

"Chase, I—" She wanted so badly to tell him. She wanted him to know what she'd done, to have him understand the success he'd achieved before she'd changed everything. Madame Claire's words hovered over her in a dire warning. Don't tell anyone or *all will unravel most unpredictably.*

He trailed a finger along her cheek. "What is it?"

A thrill shot through her at his touch. She did her best to ignore it, needing to concentrate on making him understand. "I *know* you would be successful, way more successful than me. You have to start writing again." Guilt wrapped itself around her shoulders, feeling heavier by the second. She scanned his face, looking for a sign that he would forgive her, even if he didn't know what she needed forgiveness for.

After a moment, he said, "Sometimes I wish—" He stopped.

"You wish what?" she whispered.

"We could go back." A short exhale that sounded both resigned and wistful. "To the janitor's closet."

Emma caught her breath and pulled her mouth into a smile, grasping the front of his t-shirt. "The janitor's closet."

"I know. Stupid." He shook his head, but not before she caught the look in his eye, not before she saw the memory firing there. Of the two of them. High school seniors, unable to keep their hands off each other, hiding in the janitor's closet, muffling their laughter, unable to muffle their passion.

"We were lucky Mr. Oakes was such a bad janitor," she said.

"We were lucky he spent his time smoking under the bleachers instead of going through his cleaning supplies."

Her memory caught a whiff of the solution Mr. Oakes poured in his bucket, when he remembered to mop. It had been stored in bottles on the shelves. The shelves in the dark corner where they'd used the piles of clean cloths to make a nest. A nest where they made love, their arms and legs wrapped around each other in a fiery coming together.

"We almost brought the shelf down on us once. You kicked it. Remember?" An exquisite ache had begun in her abdomen and her panties were growing damp at the flashback to the crowded closet and the pure, desperate longing for Chase that had been fulfilled in that small space, next to a shelf that held sponges, rags, and four-packs of cleanser.

His answering quiet laugh filled the stillness around them.

Emma reached up and kissed him, pulling his head forward, toward her.

Chase hesitated but then met her kiss with an urgency of his own.

His mouth on hers, bold, tender, and fierce, shut out everything else around them. She no longer knew or cared where she was, only that his kisses would never stop. Her arm snaked around his neck, holding him close; her back arched, pressing her breasts against him until she could hardly stand the need to be with him, to have him inside her once again. She moved her hand under the neck of his cotton t-shirt, reveling in the feel of his warm skin beneath her fingers.

He lifted her from the bench in one fluid move, carrying her easily in his powerful, muscled arms. He didn't break stride and they didn't break from their kisses, which had become feverish and hungry. At some point, he reached the house, kicking open the door with her in his arms.

In some remote part of her consciousness, it struck her how thrillingly *Officer and a Gentleman* that seemed, but it was nearly the last coherent thought she had as he laid her on his bed.

In the next moment, she was tugging his shirt off over his head and then he did the same with hers. Her bra was next. It sailed somewhere off into the room and her naked breasts awaited him in anticipation. Whatever words he said were lost as he buried his face between them, covering her with roughly sweet kisses. His whiskers simultaneously stung and scintillated. She caught her breath and tipped her head back, letting her hair brush against her bare back as Chase cupped and massaged her breasts with his hands.

He'd been the only one, ever, who could bring her to the place where her body took over and all else was lost.

He unzipped her jeans, tugging them off her legs and followed by doing the same with his own. His briefs were next and he stood before her, a gorgeous, sculpted, muscled man, with tan lines on his neck and arms that showed where his t-shirt had been. His penis was long and standing strong, ready and willing to do her bidding.

If only she could manage to continue breathing long enough to make that bid.

She closed her eyes, inhaled deep and opened them again. He stood at the side of the bed, over her, and hooked his finger beneath the wisp of pink fabric that served as her panties. The fabric was already soaking wet in anticipation of his touch.

Chase began stroking her, softly at first and then harder. She moaned in tortured elation and just when she was sure she could no longer stand it, he pulled her panties off and began running his tongue over her clit in rhythms that began slow and easy and moved to fast and furious as she urged him on. She came in a crescendo of agonized pleasure that left her spent and damp with sweat.

He moved up to take her in his arms and began kissing her all over, from her mouth to her breasts and down. She ran her fingers over him as tears filled her eyes, loving every inch of his familiar body. When she grasped his penis, he groaned.

And when at last he was inside her, she was certain nothing had ever felt as good or as right. They'd been apart too long. This time, they came together at once, in a shudders of passion that left them both gasping.

Either hours or no time at all had passed by the time Emma's brain cleared enough to realize that she lay in Chase's arms, wrapped in the intimacy that comes from knowing each other's bodies better than you know your own.

The sun was shining high in the sky now, streaming through the curtains in the farmhouse's sparse bedroom. An old-fashioned clock on a dark wooden dresser ticked off the seconds. Emma burrowed into Chase's arms and closed her eyes, her body and her mind sated and peaceful for the first time in months. Maybe years.

Something cold and wet nudged her back. Emma started, swallowing her scream, and turned over to see Lila the dog standing next to her, head tipped to one side. "Hi."

Chase raised his head. "What time is it?" He squinted at the clock. "Oh, Lila. Sorry, girl." He rose from the bed to open a dresser drawer and pulled out a fresh pair of briefs. "It's past her breakfast time," he explained to Emma as he went through the door of the bedroom, followed by the dog padding along behind him.

Emma smiled to herself and buried her head deeper in a pillow that smelled of detergent and fresh sunshine. She wondered if Chase hung the bedding outside to dry. She wondered if she could talk him into writing songs with her again. Making love by evening, writing by day. Or vice versa. Or both. She snickered.

A loud vibration interrupted. Her cell phone, still jammed into the pocket of her jeans. She reached over and picked up the jeans from the hardwood floor, fishing through her pockets until she found her cell. "Hello?" she said sleepily, unable to keep the happiness from spilling out of her voice. She and Chase. Together again. As they should have been all along.

"Emmy?"

"Hi, Mom." She reached for the sheet and covered up. From the direction of the kitchen, she heard the rattle of kibble hitting a bowl and Lila's approving *woof.*

"I hate to bother you when you're so busy, but the realtor said he's been trying to call and hasn't been able to get you."

Emma frowned. She'd made a point of not answering her phone while in Maven, for a reason. "What does he need?"

"I'm so sorry. I know you don't have time for this. Should I have him call your assistant, instead?"

Emma bit her lip, hanging on to her patience. Her stomach did its normal clench of muscles, expecting the worst from the conversation. "No, that's fine. I'll take care of it. Just tell me what it is."

"Something about uneven earnings. The bank needs to verify the sources of your income...or something like that, anyway."

"Okay." Emma tried to process this. She'd only ever dealt with W2s before.

"I think Jason Jeffries was supposed to sign some sort of form."

"And he hasn't done it." She had a sinking feeling. She sat up in the bed, gripping the sheet.

"I don't know for sure. But it doesn't sound like it. And they need him to."

"I'll take care of it."

"Emmy, this house is probably way too expensive. I don't know what made you think you have to buy it for me. I'm fine."

Emma stopped just short of saying, *No, you're not.* Her mother had never been fine. It was unlikely she'd start now.

"I'll call the realtor. I'll take care of this," she repeated.

"Well, if you're sure..." her mother's voice trailed away.

"I'm positive." She wasn't. Not at all. "Don't worry. I'll call you later, okay?"

Chase entered the room. Emma looked up at him, said goodbye to her mother and ended the call. She switched the phone from vibrate to ringer and laid it on the pillow next to her. If the realtor called, she'd better answer this time.

"My mother," she said to Chase.

He nodded and leaned against the doorjamb, one foot casually crossed over the other, with Lila at his side. Clad only in his briefs, with his hair at all ends, a day's growth of dark whiskers on his face, a darker tan on his lower arms and his chest bare and muscled, he had a careless, sensual handsomeness.

The lazy grin he gave her now carried a hint of vulnerability that sped her heartbeat. She had never stopped loving this man. From the high school janitor's closet to this rumpled bed in an Ohio farmhouse, she'd do anything to be with him. Stay with him.

He reached behind him to a small table and produced two mugs, steam curling from the tops. "Thought you might be ready for coffee."

She smiled. "I am."

Chase crossed the room to sit on the bed beside her. He handed her one of the cups.

She took a drink, the steam tickling her nose, and watched him over the top of the mug. "Thank you." A part of her felt shy. She looked down and pulled her shoulders in, trying to hide her smile.

"Hey." He pulled a piece of her hair away from her face. "What's with the sheet?"

She laughed, pulling it tighter, feeling shy like the teenager she'd once been.

He tugged at it. "Let's get rid of this. I like looking at you."

"Really." She did her best to infuse smoldering sexuality into the single word, but figured she was doing pretty well if she achieved a somewhat smoky playfulness.

"Really." He pulled the sheet away.

She hooked her fingers into his briefs and slowly inched over to the spot where his penis strained against the cotton. "What do we have here?"

"We have—*hell*." He set his coffee mug on the bedside table and took hers from her, placing it next to his. Then he dove toward her, wrapping her in his arms and enveloping her in a heady mix of masculinity, caffeine, naked skin, whiskers, and a rock-hard penis.

She succumbed to his hungry kisses, matching them with her own. Life did not get better. Not at this moment, maybe not ever.

The notes of a familiar tune trilled close to her head. "Wishsome." Coming from—*oh, no*. From her phone. As Chase pulled away, she scrambled to grab the phone from the pillow. He glanced at it before she could get to it.

The caller ID read *Jason*.

CHAPTER SIXTEEN

Chase's eyes darkened, his gaze holding Emma's. "Better get that."

Instead, she pressed *ignore*. "He wants lyrics." She regretted the admission as soon as it was out.

Chase sat up, rubbing his forehead. "So give him what he wants." His voice was low and controlled, but she heard anger beneath the surface.

She put a hand behind her head and looked away, toward the door. "It's not that easy." Why did Jason have to call *now*?

"Not answering his call isn't going to make it easier."

"He says we have a contract." She forced her gaze back to Chase.

He turned, meeting her eyes. A furrow appeared between his brows. "You don't know whether you have a contract?"

"No. Yes." She sucked in a breath. "I mean, I guess that yes, we have a contract."

"Turn over the lyrics, then." Chase slid out of the opposite side of the bed and stood up, grabbing his jeans and putting them on.

Emma felt as though a bright balloon she'd been holding had just eluded her grasp to slip into the sky. She wanted him back in bed, with her. About to do what they had been about to do a few minutes ago. She sat up, pressing her bare back into the wooden headboard. "I don't have them."

He turned and opened a dresser drawer, taking out a blue t-shirt. He pulled it on over his head and put his hands on hips, looking back at her. "Why?"

"I don't know." She looked down at her hands, helpless. "I haven't written anything. I don't even know where to start. It's almost like I never knew how to do this in the first place."

Silence. When she braved a look back up at him, she saw that his expression had hardened. "Did you come here thinking I would help you? Is that what this is about?"

"No!"

"Because if you're looking for a partner, that asshole's your guy. Not me. I'm nobody's second helping. And I'm *really* not going to write a song for that jerk."

"I never thought that."

"I can't believe you still want anything to do with him."

"I can't believe I'm fucking *engaged* to him!" As soon as the words were out, she wanted to scramble after them, snatch them up and stuff them back inside before he could hear.

Why, oh *why* didn't she think before she spoke?

His eyes shot sparks. "Engaged."

"Let me explain."

"Save it." He put a hand up in warning.

"It's not what you think."

"I *think* you'd better get the hell out of here." He whistled for Lila, who appeared immediately to sit at his feet, concern for her master in her eyes. "I'm serious, Emma. Be gone when I get back."

She wanted to tell him everything, confess the visit to the psychic, the do-over, all she'd done since to screw things up and mess with his life, but she couldn't. Her throat, aching and raw, swallowed anything she wanted to say.

Then he was gone. She heard the screen door at the front of the house slam. Hard. She buried her face in her hands. Of course he was furious. He thought she'd come here to either cheat on her fiancé with him or to get him to help her with lyrics she couldn't write. Or both.

Slowly, one micro-movement at a time, Emma climbed out of the bed and put on her clothes with trembling hands. When she screwed up a do-over, she screwed it up but good.

***

Every step Chase took smashed the dirt harder into the ground. She was engaged, *engaged* to that asshole.

He'd let himself take her in his arms, make love to her, let himself *feel* again what he'd once felt for her. Like a fucking idiot. It hadn't occurred to him she had an agenda.

She'd gone to all that trouble to have Beth set them up. He'd thought…*Thought* she wanted to be with him, not that she was just looking for one last screw, for old time's sake or something, before she married Jason Jeffries, big deal Nashville guy. Fuck that.

A part of his heart splintered at the betrayal, sending shards into a place that stabbed at him, over and over. Lila whimpered, as though she could tell. "It's okay, girl," he muttered.

Chase squeezed his damp eyes tight. He didn't do tears. Period. And there was no fucking way he was about to start now. He opened his eyes and stared straight ahead, concentrating on the deep green of the trees, the brown dirt of the worn path, the deep blue of the sky. He breathed in sharp and short. And out again. He could get through this; he had gotten through it the first time Emma had slashed at his heart and he could do it now.

But never again.

Then he remembered what she'd said about the lyrics she was having trouble writing and fresh pain flooded through him at the memory of her urging him to write again. Why? So she'd have songs for Jeffries?

Emma didn't know it, but he hadn't stopped writing. He couldn't do that. It would be like going without food. Nothing had come of it for several years as he mourned the death of his first partnership, but he'd decided at last to move on.

His guitars were stashed in a room in the house she hadn't seen. A part of the appeal of his grandfather's house had been the solace, the isolation, the chance to give the writing part of him serious attention again.

Zoe Webb, a damn good lyricist, had contacted him before he came here. Asked whether he'd be interested in collaborating. Zoe had just broken up with her third or thirteenth songwriting partner and was looking for someone new. She had a reputation for being difficult to work with, but she also had a Grammy for Song of the Year.

At the time, he hadn't been able to think about writing with anyone but Emma, but the more he'd thought about it, the more he'd asked himself why not. She'd left him far behind; why couldn't he do the same?

It had felt good to hold the guitar again, to let his fingers find and bring to life the melodies that were living in his head, the ones that woke him up at night and wouldn't leave until he grabbed guitar, pencil, and paper. Granted, he didn't know if he could do it, whether he could make it in the music world, but he wanted to try. That was a beginning.

He'd told Carl he wanted to cut back on doing the side gigs with the band, but he hadn't told him why: that he needed to be able to keep his promise to his parents to fix up the old place while also writing songs. Playing with a band came last.

Lila barked at a squirrel that ran across the path and up a tree. Chase bent down, picked up a stick for her to retrieve and threw it down the path with a fierceness that pulled at his shoulder muscles.

Everything had been okay, on track even, until Emma had shown up. With her eyes that made him believe they could be good together again, her soft voice that caressed him all over and her way of moving and touching him, as though she didn't know the half of what she did to him, the way his dick ached to be buried inside her when all he did was look at her.

She'd only been here a couple of days and she'd already made him believe in himself again. Believe in *them* again. He thought they'd gotten past what had happened before, that they could trust each other again.

He'd been so ridiculously excited this morning, holding her, loving her, that he'd been afraid he'd explode happiness all over. A pussy way of thinking about it, he reflected now, but it had been true.

Then.

Now the only thing he could do to save himself was hope to hell she'd be out of the house, and out of his life, before he got back.

"Come on, Lila." He picked up the pace, began walking faster, away from the old farmhouse.

He didn't want to see or hear her go for one very simple reason. He was afraid he'd go after her.

***

Emma had finally located her shoes when her phone pinged, signaling an incoming text. She picked it up. From Jason, it asked, *When do u get in today?*

She shook her head, trying to corral her thoughts, which were currently running in circles and bumping into each other with a vengeance. She texted back, *Don't know.* The truth.

Got your message. Will be at your house, waiting.

Then she remembered. She had called Jason to tell him she was coming back. Called him from the bench by the lake, when everything had gone to shit. The *first* time they'd gone to shit.

Ping. *Label is pushing up release date. Need those lyrics.*

The lyrics that would get Jason to attest to her continued earnings, so she could buy her mother a house. Emma lifted her chin. Her mother needed that house, needed to quit her job and be away from men like her "separated" boss. There was only one way that was going to happen. Through Emma.

It was roughly an eight-hour drive back to Nashville. A quick glance at the clock told her it was now just past noon. She took a deep breath and texted, *Around ten.*

Ping. *See you at your place.*

Not necessary.

Will be there anyway. Love ya.

Emma stuffed the phone into her pocket. She'd thrown away the only real love she'd known in exchange for a "touching" *love ya* from Jason Jeffries.

The only way she would get through this was to take it one step at a time. Get in the car. Get her things from the hotel. Get on the road to Nashville. Get the damn songs written.

Do, don't think. Because if she allowed herself to think about what had happened, she would dissolve into a pool of hissing, steaming liquid that would impress the Wicked Witch of the West. Right now, she was pretty sure there were people who would say she had some things in common with the almighty pointy-shoed one.

She slammed the screen door as hard as Chase had and made her way to her car, its once-shiny paint job now coated with road dirt. One step at a time, she told herself. One foot in front of the other. She didn't allow herself to look around for Chase, to hope that he'd changed his mind and come back.

Why should he? She'd just admitted to being the worst kind of cheater. He didn't know it wasn't true. He couldn't know, for fear she'd screw things up even worse than she already had.

The car rolled down the gravel path as Emma stared straight ahead with a death grip on the steering wheel. No looking right or left, no hoping she'd see him.

She turned out on the deserted main road and began accelerating, headed toward town, and repeating the steps in her head to cement them. Get things from the hotel. Get on the road to Nashville. Get the damn songs written.

A sudden flash in front of her car. A dog, frozen in the middle of the road, staring at her. Emma bit out a scream and hit the brakes.

The car swerved to one side, pitching back and forth as it traveled the shoulder and then onto a grassy area. A rock flew up and hit the passenger side with a thump before the car finally rolled to a stop.

Emma sat, hands glued to the steering wheel, her ass riveted to the seat, her mouth open. She turned back to see the dog, a black Lab, take off toward the other side of the road. Safe. Unharmed.

She turned back, realizing how lucky she was not to have been hurt. That the airbag hadn't deployed. That the car, aside from possible rock dings, didn't seem to have been affected.

Lucky. So lucky.

Her chin began to wobble uncontrollably. Her fingers released their hold on the steering wheel to join the rest of her body in shaking, from head to toe. A choked sob, then a full-out wail. She cried with her entire body, with her heart and her soul.

For Chase. For lost chances. For a do-over she'd thought was the right thing to do, for all the wrong reasons.

She didn't like what she'd found out about herself. "I'm a selfish bitch," she sobbed. She pressed her forehead to the steering wheel, feeling interminably sorry for herself, before at last raising her head. She sniffed, once and then again.

Get a grip, she scolded herself. She'd undone Chase's successful life, thinking only that she wanted another chance with him. To do what she hadn't been able to do the first time. And now, once again, she was thinking only about herself.

She had to put things back, make things right. Reaching inside her purse, she pulled out a tissue and swiped at her face. Her steps had changed.

Finding Madame Claire was now at the top of a very short list.

CHAPTER SEVENTEEN

It was a busy Saturday in the hair salon, with the high-pitched chatter of patrons nearly drowning out Bing Crosby crooning "White Christmas" as the temperature soared outside.

As soon as Emma stepped inside the door, Chrissy rushed up to her. "Thank you!" Chrissy said, grabbing Emma's hands and holding tight. "That was so great last night. And I never would have been brave enough if it hadn't been for you."

"Oh. Sure." At least she'd done one thing right. "You were great."

"I have a lot of work to do still, but I did it. I *sang* in front of people. I don't even know how to describe how it felt. It was amazing, it was—" Chrissy broke off, her excitement changing to worry. "Hey, you okay? You look terrible. Come sit down." She let go of Emma's fingers to instead put a hand on her arm and try steering her to a chair.

Emma waved her off. "I'm fine. Thanks." She squared her shoulders. "I need to talk to Mad—Um, I need Claire. Is she here?"

Chrissy's face clouded. "No. My mom decided she wasn't"— she made air quotes—"'the right fit.'" She lowered her voice to a confiding whisper. "Really, it was more like my mom *had* a fit. Claire did color on a customer, right after she saw you, and it came out orange. *Orange.* Claire tried saying she'd seen it in *Vogue*, but nobody was buying it. My mom had to take care of the woman's hair."

Emma felt a stab of pity for the psychic who had confessed to "not being a worker of hair magic," after all. Madame Claire had only been in Maven because of her misguided attempt to help Emma. "I'm sure it was just a mistake. It happens."

Chrissy rolled her eyes. "Not so sure about that, but the way she was acting toward me at Gil's was pretty rude, so I'm not sorry she's gone."

Emma frowned. "What do you mean?"

"Every time I tried to get over to talk to you and—you know, Chase, she got in front of me. I practically had to push her out of the way, but then after I did, I couldn't find him—*you*. Who does that?"

Emma chewed her lip to keep the smile from escaping. An overprotective psychic does that. She didn't say that, though, she just asked, "Do you know where I can find her?"

"I saw her going into The Blueberry earlier."

The restaurant where Emma had met Carl and Beth. "Thanks," she said, heading back toward the door.

"Emma!"

She turned back.

"I'm going to Gil's again tonight. To sing."

"Good." Emma smiled. "You should."

"Will you be there?"

"No." Just the thought made her stomach knot. "But you don't need me. You'll do great."

"Chrissy!" came a shout from the back of the salon.

"Gotta go. Good luck finding Claire. If you still want to, that is."

"Thanks." Emma sighed. She needed more than luck. She went out the door, headed in the direction of the heavenly smelling blueberry pancakes.

The restaurant was only half full at this time of day. Emma immediately spotted Madame Claire in a corner, staring down at a plate with a half-eaten egg and a piece of toast. A minute later, Emma had slid into the seat opposite her, taking care to avoid the rip in the vinyl that had been patched with duct tape.

Madame Claire looked up in surprise. "What is it you are doing here?" She gestured at Emma. "Looking like this?"

No point in answering that question. Emma had one of her own. "What did your mother tell you to do, you know, to fix things?"

The other woman looked around them nervously, but no one was sitting close enough to hear their conversation. "That woman, my mother, she is of the mind that there is only one way ever to do something. Her own daughter she criticizes. It is most irritating."

"She said you got it wrong. That something was missing."

"What can I say, she calls at three a.m., thinking it is nothing better I have to do than hear her with the scolding. A person must sleep." She tucked a piece of blue-streaked silver hair behind her ear and stabbed at the egg on her plate with a fork.

"But you *told me* you got it wrong."

Another fierce stab with the fork, which this time sent the egg skittering off the plate and onto the red table. The psychic picked it up with her fingers and plopped it back on the plate, wiping rubbery yolk from her fingers with a paper napkin. "No person is perfect," she said.

A piece of red lipstick had transferred to Madame Claire's front tooth. Emma thought about pointing it out, but decided against changing the subject.

"Believe me, I know that." Emma shook her head. "I'm not accusing you of anything. I just want to know what your mother said to do to fix it. Because my do-over isn't going well. At all."

Madame Claire's dark eyes softened. "It is sorry I am to know that. Perhaps it is all a part of the journey. What is now so will not always be so."

It sure felt as though it would always be so, unless there was some sort of an emergency spell patch. Emma propped her chin in her hand and stared over Madame Claire's shoulder at the restaurant's counter. A lone customer perched on the bar stool, taking a drink from his cup of coffee and setting it back down on the Formica. He lifted his fork and knife and dug into a fresh stack of pancakes.

Emma's stomach rumbled its envy at the sight. She ignored it. "I wish that were true," Emma said. "But I don't see how it can be."

The psychic sighed. "My mother, she was good at this. Did not make such mistakes. Of which she always reminds me."

"She did this kind of thing, too?"

"And her mother before her. Not many times, you must know. But enough. Do you think Eleanor chose to marry her cousin the first time around? No. But in the end, it was good for all in this country that she chose a different action when the chance, it came upon her."

Emma stared as the psychic's words sank in. She thought back to her history lessons. "Eleanor Roos—?"

"We must not speak names. Of this, I will be most strict."

"*You* just spoke a name."

For the first time since Emma had known her, Madame Claire appeared flustered. "You are not to mind that."

Okay, she wouldn't mind that. "Back to your mother," Emma said. "You still haven't told me what she said would fix things. I can't imagine she called you up and didn't have an opinion."

Very carefully, Madame Claire folded the yolk-stained paper napkin and placed it on her plate, which she pushed away from her. "The problem, it is that you remember what came before."

"Yes," Emma agreed. "I remember that Chase was a very successful songwriter before I messed everything up for him by having you give me a do-over."

"This is not healthy, this blame you are taking." The silver head bobbed, emphasizing her point. "You must remember that it is how things unfolded with other choices made." She sighed. "It is simple. If I had said all of the words, *if* my mother is correct, you would know nothing else. There would be no blame because it is nothing else you would know. So the problem, it is in your mind, where your…" she made a circular motion around the top of her own head, "…memories are mixing around."

"I understand that," Emma said, willing to look as if she did if it took the psychic to the problem-solving part of the conversation. "What I want to know now is how we fix it."

"I do not profess to understand why we must." Madame Claire squared her shoulders. "All will proceed as it should. It is different now, but that is life, is it not?"

The woman's hand trembled, Emma noticed. "Are you scared to try to change it?"

Madame Claire made a dismissive *pffft* sound. "Scared. I do not know the meaning of the word." An undercurrent of something that sounded a lot like fear ran through the bold words. She brushed crumbs from her skirt and made a move toward her purse.

Emma slid her hand across the table toward the psychic. "It's okay if you are. I understand. This is scary stuff."

Madame Claire hesitated and then folded her arms in front of her on the table, her many bracelets clinking against the wood in alarm.

"You came all the way here to help me," Emma said. "I'm guessing you don't do that very often."

"It was clear you were in need of the help." She lifted her chin.

"I was. I am. And I appreciate it."

The psychic looked away and then back at Emma. "It is perhaps possible I do not know what would happen should I attempt a change."

Emma sat back against the chair. "We didn't know what would happen the first time, either."

"My mother, she scolds, but also she says I could reverse."

"Reverse the spell?"

"Yes."

"So that everything would go back to the way it was. Before."

"Indeed. She is in favor of this."

"And you?"

"I do not know. I think perhaps it is that I should stay and make things for the better."

Emma shook her head. "I don't know that you can. That anyone can make them better." Her voice caught, the admission harder than even she had thought it would be.

Madame Claire leaned forward, dropping her voice to a stage whisper. "There are things that can be done. To make him in love with you."

Emma's eyes went wide. "No."

"Yes. Such a spell, *that* is simple. He need never know."

"I won't do that." With her life upside down, she didn't know a lot, but she knew she wasn't going to have Madame Claire work Chase over with a love spell. "That wouldn't be real love. He would only love me because you made him. And I would always know it."

The psychic lifted a shoulder. "Sure, it is so. But is the end not worth the beans?"

Emma blinked, not understanding. "Beans?" Had the woman misunderstood the saying, means to an end?

Madame Claire made an exasperated sound. "The spell, it uses beans. I believe it is chili beans you call them. Why is it no one understands this?" She raised her palms, imploring the heavens, and then began speaking in another language. Emma didn't understand what she said, but suspected it had something to do with asking questions of the universe.

"*No* love spell," she said. "No beans."

"But if it is love you seek—"

"Not like that."

"As you wish," the woman huffed.

"So all that's on the table is a reversal. Everything goes back the way it was before I came to see you."

Madame Claire looked confused. "All that is on the table is eggs." She turned to look over her shoulder. "And toast, with too much of the burning. The waitress, I do not know where she is."

Emma did. The waitress had been chatting up the customer at the counter for the last fifteen minutes.

"Ah, there," Madame Claire said. "She raised her hand to wave.

Emma reached up to put the other woman's hand down. "Don't call her over, yet. I need to think."

"It is the burned toast I must look at while you think?"

"It is." This wasn't an easy decision. On one hand, if she did a reversal, Chase would go back to being a happy, super-successful songwriter. Wait. Had he *looked* happy in that magazine article she'd read? Zoe Webb had looked happy. Chase had looked impassive. Content, though. And why wouldn't he be? It was everything he'd ever dreamed of.

On the other hand, Emma would go back to being an out-of-work music teacher. Unable to give her mother the financial security she'd always needed. In this new life, her mother actually listened to her instead of to the men who promised her everything she wanted to hear and never came through with any of it.

Her stomach clenched in a mixture of love, resentment, and obligation. Emma was the only child her mother had, the only one who could and would watch out for her. It should have been the other way around, but it never had been.

"Perhaps it would be best to speak your thinking."

Emma looked up to see Madame Claire's gaze filled with concern. "Thanks, but I don't think so." How could she explain years of family drama to someone she barely knew?

Bells above the door of the restaurant jingled. "You found her." Chrissy approached their table, a new swagger in her step.

"I did."

The gazes of Chrissy and Madame Claire met and bounced off each other. If they had been boxers, Emma thought, they would have been circling each other, deciding who would throw the first punch.

"Well, I just wanted to be sure," Chrissy said. "I have to get back to the salon."

"Thanks." Emma lifted her hand.

Madame Claire sniffed, as though Chrissy were beneath her level of attention.

Once the bells over the door had put an exclamation point on Chrissy's departure, Emma said, "She's not so bad."

"A shampoo girl, she is."

"She wants more. She can sing."

"If sing she must, it should be as she shampoos. 'Frosty the Snowman,' she should sing." Madame Claire chortled.

"You can't hold her responsible for her mother's musical preferences. And what's wrong with being a shampoo girl? She works hard."

"You are being most unwise."

"You are being most judgmental."

"This Chase of yours, it is him she wants. You must see that."

Emma was done with the conversation, done with thinking. "If he wants her, maybe *that's* what is supposed to be."

"You do not mean this."

She did mean it, though. She only wanted Chase if he wanted her. And not through some love spell that used chili beans. Her head hurt. Her stomach hurt. Her heart hurt. And the only thing she knew for sure was that she wanted out of this conversation and out of this restaurant. "I'm leaving." She stood.

"You cannot."

"I have to. I'm going back to Nashville."

"But the one you love, he is here!" Madame Claire protested.

"He knows where to find me. If he wants to."

The psychic clutched at Emma's arm. "You must please to let me help you."

"Tell your mother it wasn't your fault. You did your best." Emma bent to give Madame Claire a quick hug, inhaling exotic flowers, incense, and tobacco.

The other woman did not return the hug, but as Emma turned to leave, Madame Claire called to her. "Come, please. You will come."

Emma took the few steps back and the psychic reached an arm around Emma's neck, patting her hard on the shoulder. "There. You go now."

"Sorry about your mother's call tonight. I'm sure it won't be good."

"Well." She pulled a tissue from a giant purse and pressed it to her nose. "That is not of your concern." She dug around more in her purse, producing a small piece of paper and a pen. After scrawling numbers on it in black ink, she handed it to Emma. "My number. You need it, you will call."

"Thank you." Emma tucked it in her jeans pocket. She wouldn't call.

"But not to give it to anyone else."

Oh hell, no.

CHAPTER EIGHTEEN

It was nearly midnight by the time Emma reached her house in Nashville. As she pulled up in front, a feeling of satisfaction unexpectedly washed over her. She might not be able to remember all the details of the renovation she'd supposedly done, but a part of her felt as though she knew and treasured every inch of the house's restored glory.

She'd always wanted to take on a project like that. Apparently, she had.

She climbed from the leather driver's seat, overnight bag in hand. Her shoes whispered quick steps on the red brick walkway as she approached the door. It opened easily in her hand.

Inside, Jason rose from a white sofa, laying a magazine on a table. "You're back." His cowboy hat rested on a sofa cushion, looking as untouched as if it had just been removed from plastic. It was unnatural, Emma decided. Normal people acquired a few dents along the way.

She closed the door behind her but didn't move from the entry.

He strode over to fold her in a big hug. Then he dropped a kiss on her cheek. "I brought wine. I'll pour you a glass."

"That would be nice. Thanks." Emma dropped her bag with a thud.

"Where were you?" Jason asked as he produced and opened a bottle, poured her a glass of red wine, and held it out to her.

She took it. "I needed time. Away."

"Good." He stared at her fireplace and took a long sip from his glass of wine. "That's good." He made it sound anything but. "Come sit." He dropped back onto the sofa. "Tell me about it."

The last thing she wanted to do was tell Jason anything about her time in Maven. With Chase.

She pushed his cowboy hat to one side and sank onto the cushion next to him, taking another bolstering drink of wine. "Nothing much to tell. Just had to take care of a few things. So your release date has been pushed up. Why?"

He shrugged. "Got me. But when the label says this is the date, you say, yes sir, that is the date. They're linin' up a tour to go along with it. Should be good."

"That's great."

"Yeah." He ran a hand through his hair, somehow managing to not disturb a single strand. "Gotta get into the studio and put down those last three tracks, though." Draining his glass, he set it on the table and reached over to grab a guitar leaning across the wall. "Brought this baby with me, so all we need are your lyrics and we can get to work."

"Right now?"

A flash of white teeth. "Right now."

Alarm pitted in her stomach. He'd find out for sure. Find out that she didn't even know how to write anymore. She couldn't do this with him watching. Waiting. "The thing is…they're not ready yet."

Jason strummed a chord, pulling his mouth into a grimace. When he turned to meet her gaze, his brown eyes had narrowed. "The thing is, that doesn't work for me."

"I'm sorry." She was.

"That's great and all, but I'm sorry does not a song make."

"I told you I would have lyrics for you and I will. At the end of the week."

"The end of the week." His tone was flat.

"That's what I said. Thank you for making sure I got home okay. And for bringing wine. It was so nice. Really. But now, if it's okay with you, I just need to get some sleep." She was exhausted, from her pinky toes all the way up. All she wanted was to have the house to herself so she could figure out how she was going to write the lyrics to three songs. In five days.

She put her glass of wine on the table and pushed herself up from the sofa. He grabbed the neck of his guitar and followed suit.

By the time she'd rounded the sofa to move toward the door and show him out, he'd come around the other side to stand in front of her, blocking her way.

"I'll have them, Jason," she repeated. "I promise." If she had to write a country version of 'Twinkle, Twinkle Little Star,' she'd give him something. "Good night." She made a move to go around him to open the door.

He reached out to grab her arm. "Not so fast."

"What are you doing?" She looked down in disbelief. "Let go of me."

He didn't. "Not until you start writing."

"Who the hell do you think you are? You don't get to threaten me."

A vein in Jason's neck jumped. "You're forgetting we have a contract."

"Pretty hard to forget that. You won't let me."

Jason's expression hardened. One of his eyebrows started to twitch. "The bank called me today."

"I heard."

"You wanna buy your mama that house?"

She pulled her mouth tight.

"What I tell them tomorrow depends on what you do tonight." He leaned in closer.

She drew away. *Come on, new Emma. Show the hell up and help me take care of this asshole.*

"So sit down and let's get to makin' some music. Once I have my songs, I'll talk to the bank and you'll have your loan. I don't get my songs, and…" his voice turned into a croon that nauseated her. "Well, we don't want to go there."

That was it. She'd had enough. This country Ken doll wannabe did not get to issue Emma Zane an ultimatum. Her fist clenched at the same time her teeth did. "Let. Me. Go."

He released her, staring at the pink marks on her arm, surprise flickering across his face. "Hey, I didn't mean to—"

She growled, "Get your guitar and get the fuck out of my house before I call the police."

"Hold on." He began backing up, his palms in the air. "I said I didn't mean to," he protested. "I just need those songs. You know that."

"The only thing I know is that, if you ever touch me again, my first call is to the police and my second call is to a reporter."

"If I ever *touch* you again? We're engaged!"

"Not anymore." She shook her head. "My standards just got a whole lot higher. And you don't even come close."

He gaped. "What about the ring? The record release?"

"If that's all you're worried about, you'll find someone else to marry you in five minutes."

"Emma." Whining turned his voice nasal. "You know that's not all I'm worried about. I'm worried about *you*. I love you. You love me."

"Don't think so." She moved around him to open the front door, her eyes widening and her chin tipped meaningfully at the summer night that waited outside.

"I got carried away," he pleaded. "I was trying to make you understand. You took off without telling me where you were going. Now you don't have those lyrics…and I don't know, I guess I got scared." His perfect nose quivered. Sweat broke out on his forehead.

"Last warning." She pointed out at the door. "Don't make me throw you out. Never know what might happen to your hat."

He clutched the hat closer, as though worried she'd make good on the threat. Then he fled. A real cowboy would have described him as a lily-livered pond-sucker.

As she slammed the door and locked it behind him, she wasn't sure if it was new Emma she had to thank or if old Emma had finally come to her senses and stood up for herself. She guessed it didn't matter. He still held the cards because he held the contract. But for tonight, anyway, she'd kicked Jason's sorry ass to the curb.

And it felt good. Real good.

***

Emma sat cross-legged on the floor of her home office, surrounded by notebooks stacked and scattered at all angles, some of them with crinkled pages. She'd found at least thirty so far, all of them spiral bound and college ruled. Inside she'd found lyrics in her handwriting. Most were scrawled, as if she'd been in a hurry, a few were neatly written.

Some entries were terrible, some had real possibilities, and a few hit home, touching her heart in ways she could feel, but not quite remember. When she read one, tears pricked behind her eyes. Another sent a wave of nostalgia through her.

Harder, though, were the notebooks holding verses that were clearly about Chase. Poignant words about their relationship, from the joy of an intimate connection of two hearts on a shared journey to the pain of misunderstanding, accusations, and loss. *You're the life in my love*, she had written in one. *The beat of my heart, my soul's energy.*

In later pages, the lyrics changed to a sadness that leapt from the pages, wrapping itself around Emma and clinging to her in a plea for sympathy. She shook her head at the depth of despair, her only thought that she was glad she must have fought her way through it, despite the scars that remained.

Subsequent notebooks dealt with love and loss on a less intense, more commercial level.

It was a strange, fascinating and empty sensation. All at the same time. A lot like experiencing the thrill of accepting a prestigious award without being able to remember how she'd earned it.

Madame Claire's dead mother had offered a key to unlock that part of her brain. Maybe she needed to take it.

Noooooo. She squeezed her eyes tight and opened them again. If she did that, she'd lose the memories of her and Chase together at the farmhouse that now lived inside her heart, giving her the strength she needed to make it through another baffling day. No one could touch those memories; she wouldn't let them.

Back to work.

Sun streamed through the window, casting its rays across the rug. Emma thought back to the snippets she remembered from Jason talking about his record's theme. *It's about home,* he'd said. *And making it big.*

Two very different themes. Maybe home and family as a foundation for making it big? She imagined a row of big and small Jasons and Jason-ettes, perfect from head to toe. They didn't look like the supportive type of family.

Something else, then. She wondered what the other songs were about. Another phrase he'd said flashed into her mind, something about *bigger than love.* At the time, she'd wanted to ask him what could be bigger than love. Now that she knew him a little better, she might be able to answer that. Charts, awards, fans, fame. Oh—and immovable hair that didn't dent when a cowboy hat hit it.

Emma shook her head. Could be a good thing she'd shown up to knock some sense into new Emma, who had been ready to settle for a guy who bought hair spray by the gallon. She shuddered.

Still, songs were due and songs would be written. She chewed on the end of a pencil, thinking. Jason Jeffries seemed to have room in his life for only one person to love—himself.

So she'd write him a song about that. She opened a notebook and turned to an empty white page. Using the freshly sharpened end of the pencil, she began writing phrases and snippets, filling up several pages with lines. Then she went back and crossed out most of them, leaving only a few.

A while later, she had a dulled pencil and a verse she was sure would go straight over Jason's inflated head.

There's only room for one in my pickup truck
'Cause baby, I'm headed home
And I'm up on my luck

She snickered to herself as she wrote the rest of the lyrics, about a guy returning to his small town for fanfare and a parade in his honor, with an ego so large he couldn't fit anyone else in his prized new truck.

Subtlety was the key, she decided, so she made sure the words told the story from the character's point of view in a playfully naïve sort of way, as if he didn't even realize what he was saying. Which she hoped Jason wouldn't.

At the end of a few hours, she was pleased with the final result and even more excited that she'd been able to turn out a full set of lyrics to a song. She could do this. Probably. Maybe. No, she really could.

Looking through another notebook, she found a verse that made her laugh because it fit right into Jason's theme, though maybe not as he'd originally intended. The title: *Home is where the K-Mart is.*

She spent the rest of the afternoon rhyming, chuckling, second-guessing herself, celebrating, agonizing, and sweating it out as she wrote lyrics to the song. Why had she ever chosen a career that demanded and took so much from her? She hated songwriting. And she loved every minute of it.

So life was complicated.

As the afternoon sun yielded to early evening, Emma stretched her back out by lying on the floor, arms out to her sides, staring up at the exposed wooden beams of the ceiling. Strong, sturdy and built to withstand the ravages of time, they had to be original to the home. She was glad she'd left them there.

Wait a minute. That gave her an idea. For lyrics.

But these lyrics…she wasn't about to let Jason Jeffries have. She shot back upright and grabbed a new pencil and a fresh page in the notebook.

CHAPTER NINETEEN

Emma pushed the heel of her hand to her forehead and the small of her back into the chair. Then she breathed in deep and let her gaze again land on Jason, his back hunched over his guitar and his expression growing fiercer by the minute.

She was beginning to understand why he'd insisted on her being with him when he wrote music for the lyrics she'd handed him the day before. He needed help. Big-time. The melodies he came up were not only simple, but also boring. And the chord changes didn't fit.

The more time that passed, the more frustrated he became. While Emma could tell when something wasn't right, she wasn't a lot of help with suggestions on how to fix it.

At one point, he took things up an octave, for no discernible reason. When she asked him why, he snapped, "Because my voice has range and I want to show it."

At the expense of the song? She wondered how in the hell they'd managed to turn out a hit like "Wishsome." Had to have been a lucky accident.

They had claimed an empty room in the record label's massive building to write the three remaining songs Jason needed. If nothing else, legendary musical memories should have been seeping through the walls, the floor, and the ceiling, to help them get to greatness.

So far, it wasn't happening. All legendary music appeared to have fled to safer ground.

"Take another shot at it," she said, her voice more calm than she felt. "What if you start the chorus out low? And hold that note at the end?"

"What if you give me lyrics I can fucking work with?" he shot back.

Her heart sank. She was a lousy songwriter; she'd known it all along. Her throat tightened as she visualized her life going downhill, her and her mom back in some faceless, lifeless apartment as she searched for a job to support them. A familiar panic began to ripple through her at the thought of being out of work and out of options.

The purchase of her mother's new house was scheduled to close in two weeks. She couldn't back out now; her mom had already invited everyone she knew over to see the place and bragged about her daughter buying it for her.

She didn't want to be the kind of daughter who promised and then backed out of things. Too many people had done that to her mother, and Emma wasn't about to be one of them.

Jason rubbed the back of his neck and looked away, toward the door. "Sorry," he mumbled.

"It's okay," she said to the floor, feeling a flush steal over her cheeks. "Sorry I didn't give you something better to work with."

"The lyrics aren't the problem," announced a male voice behind them.

Startled, Emma turned to see a slight man with round glasses standing in the doorway. She hadn't heard him open the door. He looked like a science teacher she'd once known, as though everything on his face, from his nose to his chin and cheeks, had been pinched hard and the skin hadn't yet relaxed.

"Isn't that right, Jason?"

Emma looked back at her one-time fiancé, who was busy scowling at the wall. "We don't need you, *Bob*." He spat out the man's name. Jason's features didn't look quite so country-cover-model when he was angry.

The man moved through the room to take a seat at a piano in the corner. He crossed his legs and put his hands on his knees, attention focused on Jason. "Right," he said. "Hand 'em over."

Jason's face turned red. "I'm doing these songs myself."

"That is not going to happen."

"You're not calling the shots here." Jason pulled out his cell, fumbling to find a number. "I'm calling my agent."

"Go ahead," Bob said, unfazed. "He'll tell you the same thing. No throwaway songs, just because you would like to think you can write music. I'll put music to these, the same way I always do."

Jason stood up, kicking over his chair in the process. It thumped and skidded on the wooden floor. "Go to hell, Bob."

"Sure thing. See you there."

Jason's jaw worked furiously before he strode to the door, a death grip on the neck of his guitar, and disappeared through it. The door slammed behind him.

Bob waited a minute and then followed, opening the door to look both ways down the hall before shutting it again quietly. He looked at Emma. "And the tantrum has begun," he observed, adjusting his glasses, which had slipped down his nose. "Artists." He shook his head. "Now may I see the lyrics, please?"

"Of course." Emma stood, scrambling to collect them. A few of the pages fell from her lap, scattering to rest on the floor a couple of feet away. Gathering them up gave her a chance to peer at the man sitting at the piano. So *he'd* been the one to write the music for "Wishsome"?

"Here you go," she said, handing him the pages of lyrics for the three songs.

He scanned them, alternately frowning and smiling. She waited, swallowing hard. What if he called her out as a fraud, a hack writer, reporting her to the Country Music Association as a person who could not possibly have deserved their award? She pictured men in cowboy hats and suits, showing up at her door to demand its return.

Footsteps sounded outside the door, paused, and continued on, fading away. A page rustled as Bob set it aside and went on to the next.

Emma waited, holding her breath.

"Good," he said at last.

"Really?" Emma exhaled.

He looked up at her, brows furrowed, as though surprised by her response. "Yes. I like the hook in this one," he jabbed a finger at the paper, "and the chorus in this one."

"That's—wonderful!" Emma bounded up from her chair. Relief nearly buckled her body, but she recovered quickly, pumping her fist in the air.

Bob disregarded his slipping glasses to look over them and up at Emma. "Don't tell me you were relying on Jason's opinion."

Oh. Uh. "He is the one singing."

"He has a good voice. No, an excellent one. He's good looking, an adequate guitarist and he can carry off the perception he wrote the music. That's all the label needs from him."

"He just won Songwriter of the Year, with me."

Now Bob looked concerned. "I thought you were fine with that. You signed the confidentiality agreement, just like Jason did." He swiveled on the piano bench to face Emma. "Are you changing your mind now, with this new record?"

So this man was undercover, sent in by the label to rescue songs. That would be the only reason for a confidentiality agreement. "No." At least she didn't think so. "But the award—I earned it, right? 'Wishsome.' The lyrics were mine." She mentally crossed her fingers, hoping against hope he wouldn't correct her.

"Yes, the lyrics were yours." He looked puzzled.

"Thank you." She kept her face impassive, even though a brass band had started up inside her, complete with smiling baton twirlers. "Um…so which one would you like to start with?" She raised her voice to overcome the joyful trumpet player in her head. The drum major began high-stepping to the skies.

"What's with all this insecurity, all of a sudden? Like you said, you just won a major award. What happened, all the hoopla go to your feet instead of your head?" He chuckled at his own joke.

Whoops. Old Emma, the one who knew she hadn't written lyrics for a long time, was letting her insecurities come out to play. "Never mind. I don't know what's wrong with me today." She shook her head and widened her eyes, did everything but slap her forehead with her hand.

He didn't go for it, but appeared ready to move on. "I'll start playing with some music for the chorus of this one," he said, finger to his chin, "and I'm thinking on this other one…" He picked up the sheet of lyrics for the one she'd written about Jason and his inflated ego. "What if the guy is singing about a girl here?"

"Oh." She moved to look over his shoulder at the words.

"Don't get me wrong. It's Jason Jeffries, for sure." He paused, looking up at her, "but I don't think the label's going to like it. Too close to home in his case. Plus, it's not really something people would want to sing along with. You know what I mean?"

Emma ducked her chin. "I get it." The words might have gone over Jason's head, but Bob saw them for exactly what they were.

"Maybe you twist it some. It's a girl the guy's always wanted, since high school or something, and she becomes a big deal and is headed back to her hometown. He thinks she's going to have this giant ego and he still won't be able to get near her and surprise, she doesn't. Not only that, but she's always wanted to be with him. Last chorus is something around him discovering there's room for him in her pickup truck and now *he's* up on his luck."

"I like it." Bob was right. She should have been thinking more about audience appeal than about sticking it to Jason. Although, in retrospect, writing those words had been highly therapeutic. "I can do that."

"Great. Why don't you bring them back in the next week or so and we'll have another look. Meanwhile, I'll get started putting music to this one."

Emma tipped her head to one side. "Will that give him enough time, with the release date being moved up?"

Bob put his hands on the keyboard and began playing a few soft notes. "Jason's the only one who wanted it moved up. And that was because he wanted to get those songs done before the label had time to send me in. I was working on something else, but I finished up early."

Puzzle pieces were falling into place, one by one. "I see," Emma said, nodding.

"They're sticking with the original date."

"Okay, then." Emma walked over to the chair to gather up her things. Bob continued playing, his eyes on her handwritten lyrics.

She had her hand on the doorknob when he stopped her. "Hey," he called.

"Yes?"

"Congratulations on the award. You deserved it. You're damn good."

She flushed, warmed all over by the praise. "Thank you." She hesitated. "But don't you feel, I don't know, cheated? You wrote 'Wishsome,' too. *You* deserved the award, not Jason."

Regret flashed across his face so quickly, she nearly didn't catch it. It was replaced by an impassive look. "It's enough that I know that; no one else needs to."

She took a step toward the older man, not sure she believed him. "I'll always know how good you are."

He smiled. "Thank you. Now get out of here and let me work. We have hits to make."

Hits. With her lyrics. "Yes, sir." She flung open the door, the smile on her face stretching from one side to the other.

She practically danced along the long hallway. A female Kevin Bacon in the barn. Then, halfway down, she pulled to an abrupt halt, the pages of lyrics again falling from her hands, this time to gracefully fly through the air before landing on the floor a few feet away.

Chase.

He stopped.

They stared at each other.

The members of the brass band in Emma's brain ran into each other and fell down in a clatter of bleating horns.

"Emma."

"What are you doing here?"

Before he could reply, a woman with long red hair bounded up from behind him to lay a hand on his arm. The polish that sparkled on her fingernails looked suspiciously like Emma's favorite—Sing Me Crazy Red. "Hey, got us a room," she said to Chase.

Emma's mouth opened. Nothing came out.

"Emma, this is Zoe Webb." Chase gestured between the two of them. "She went to find us an empty space." He cleared his throat and crossed his arms. "To work on some songs."

"Oh. Sure." Zoe Webb. The woman from the magazine article she'd read before going to Madame Claire's in Seattle. Chase and Zoe had been called the hottest songwriting duo in country music.

More gesturing from Chase. "Zoe, this is Emma Zane."

"Oh, we know each other," Zoe said brightly. "Congratulations on your CMA award, by the way. 'Wishsome' was, you know, great." Her smile glittered. "I'll get you next time."

Emma rarely disliked someone right away, but it turned out Zoe Webb was the exception to the rule. "Thanks." She glittered, or more accurately, *gritted* her own smile right back. "Chase, can I talk with you for a minute?"

"Oh, wish he could," Zoe purred, "but if we don't get into that room right now, we're going to lose it."

"I'll be right there."

"Nope. Somebody else was trying to get in there already." Zoe's voice was firm. "Come on. Now, before I change my mind." She turned around, pulling him with her.

Chase shook off her hand. "You go," he said to Zoe. "Hold room."

Zoe's face clouded, but she did as he said, flouncing down the hall in her tight jeans and stilettos. "Make sure it's only a minute," she called. "I don't have all day, you know."

When she'd disappeared, Emma said, "You're writing again."

He looked down at his boots. "I never stopped."

"I'm glad." The words were inadequate and she was now someone who came up with words for a living. The irony made her cringe. "So, Zoe Webb. She's good."

"She is. Not like—" He stopped. "But yeah. And you're here writing with what's-his-name?"

"I am. Well, sort of, anyway."

His brow crinkled. "Good luck. Hope that means another hit for you."

"Thanks." The awkwardness between them, the words that hovered in the air unspoken, were almost more than she could bear.

"I'd better get back to Zoe." He jerked his thumb in the direction the other woman had gone. "She's not known for her patience."

Their gazes locked and she could have sworn the air between them crackled. She took a step forward. He took a step forward. And then a door opened down the hall and, zap, it was gone and they were back to the safety of politeness.

"Gotta go," he said.

"I know."

He hesitated and then turned away.

"Chase."

He looked back.

"I'm not engaged. I'm not going to be Mrs. What's-his-name." She felt out of breath after she said it.

His brows drew together and then smoothed. He nodded. "Good. He wasn't the one for you."

No, he wasn't, Emma thought. *The one for me is walking down the hall to another woman.*

***

Chase wasn't paying attention, an unforgiveable mistake where Zoe Webb was concerned.

"Hey!" She snapped her fingers in front of his face. "Did you hear me?"

"Sorry. Yes." No, he hadn't. Seeing Emma in the hallway like that had thrown him. He'd hated how they'd talked to each other, as if they were acquaintances instead of two people who had once shared everything.

"You want to work this out on the guitar or the piano?"

He looked up, knowing the guilt of not listening was written all over his face. "Guitar."

She sat back. "Tell me what's going on."

"Nothing." She wasn't engaged to that asshole. Had she broken things off after the time they spent at the farmhouse? Because of what had happened between them?

Didn't matter. Once again, she hadn't told him everything and he wasn't going down that road again. Ever. It wasn't lost on him that both times, Jason Jeffries had been involved. The guy needed some pieces of his face rearranged.

He grabbed his guitar. "I'm ready."

He bent over it, staring at the words Zoe had printed out and placed on the table. Black ink on white paper, Arial font. Clean, sterile. His mind flashed back to the way Emma wrote out her lyrics, by hand, in spiral bound notebooks. Any given page usually had at least one coffee stain and maybe a smear of dark chocolate.

The woman liked her caffeine.

Fuck. Thoughts of Emma were stuck like glue to his brain. He began to strum, hunting for a melody, hoping to unstick the pieces. And hoped to hell he didn't run into her again in the hall.

His cell vibrated. He pulled it from his pocket to check the caller ID. Carl.

"I'm sorry," he apologized to Zoe. "I have to take this."

"Now?" Zoe rolled her eyes. "If we ever get any work done, I'm going to be amazed."

"I'll be right back. Promise."

"I'll be waiting." She lifted an eyebrow and crossed her legs, letting one shoe dangle from her foot.

It was either a ploy to get him back in the room as soon as possible or an open invitation. Zoe was one hot woman, but her timing sucked. The last time he'd had a relationship with a songwriting partner, things hadn't turned out so great. Shit. Emma was still stuck in his brain, but now it was more like super glue.

He put his guitar down and answered the call as he moved toward the door. "Carl. What's goin' on?" Chase ducked through the door and closed it behind him.

His friend's voice was a few decibels louder than normal. "Guess what, I'm a Dad!" he shouted, following the announcement with throaty laughter.

Chase held the phone away from his ear and grinned. "That's great. Congratulations!"

"You should see her. She's beautiful!"

"A girl." He pictured Carl and Beth holding their baby. "That's so cool. How's Beth doing?"

"Good, good. She's good. Tired, you know, and all. The baby came early, but it took a long time. Twenty hours or twenty-eight hours or somethin' like that."

"So you didn't get much sleep."

"Hell, no. She kept grabbin' me around the neck and tellin' me to wake up or she'd make sure I could never father a kid again."

Chase laughed. It felt rusty, as though it had been way too long since he'd laughed. "Good thing you did what she told you to."

"I'm pretty sure she would have done it, too," Carl said, sounding in awe. "Never seen her like that before. Didn't make that mistake again. From then on, I was awake. Afraid to close my eyes."

"Text me a picture."

"I will, I will. But first— hold on a minute." Chase heard noise in the background, the sound of footsteps, voices and then the sound of something screeching across the floor. "I'll take her," he heard Carl say. And then another voice came on the line.

"Hi, Chase," Beth said. "Did you hear the news?" She sounded tired, but giddy.

"Carl told me. Congratulations. You guys will be great parents." They deserved every bit of the happiness he could hear coming from the other end of the phone.

"Pretty wild, huh? We have a girl. A *daughter*."

"It's great," Chase agreed. "I'm happy for you."

"We named her Leah. Carl says he's never going to let her date. Or not until she's thirty, anyway."

"Sounds about right."

"Speaking of which…" Beth's voice turned serious. "You want to tell me what happened with you and Emma?"

"No." He did not. "Nothing happened. So tell me about the baby." He racked his brain for a question to ask about an infant, something that would take Beth's mind off of him and Emma, a place he did not want to go. "Does she, uh, have hair?"

"Yes," Beth replied firmly. "Lots of it. My hair. Carl's nose, which is too bad, but plastic surgeons aren't *that* expensive."

Chase heard Carl protest in the background.

"Oh, shut up," Beth said to him fondly. "I love your nose and you know it." She turned her attention back to Chase. "I want to know why Emma blew out of town like that. Jen at the hotel said she couldn't leave fast enough and she looked like she'd been crying. What did you do?"

There were drawbacks, big ones, to living in a small town. He thought back to the anonymity of Seattle with a sudden longing. "It's a long story."

"So you knew each other before. Blah, blah, blah. She should have told me that, but I'll find out later why she didn't. Now we're through that part of the story, so it's not such a long one. Wait— hold on. Carl, support her *head*."

He heard his friend say that he was doing exactly that. Then Beth was back on the line. "Chase. Get to the part where you screwed things up."

"What makes you think we didn't meet for the first time when you introduced us?"

Beth made a sound of derision. "I know everything. Quit changing the subject."

Chase wasn't falling for that; he remained silent. Beth would be a formidable mother. She had a way of making people think she knew things she didn't. Until they told her.

"Okay, so I asked her," Beth admitted after a minute. "After I saw the way you looked at her. Anybody could see you already knew each other. And not in the oh-hey-it's-great-to-see-you-again kind of way."

Chase closed his eyes and turned toward the wall, resting a fist against it. "Look, it didn't work out. Then or now. I'm sorry if that screws up the video for your business. You can set me up with somebody else and do another one." His chest began to ache at the thought.

"In your dreams," Beth snapped. "I'm not setting you up with anyone else. Ever again."

"Great." Made it easy for him. "Fine with me."

"Because if you don't go after that girl, Chase Chapman, and make whatever you did wrong right, you are the biggest idiot I've ever known and I will personally see to it you never date anyone ever again."

Chase had a sinking feeling he knew why Carl had stayed awake for so many hours at Beth's command. The woman had a way with a threat. And Chase wasn't even married to her.

"What makes you think she wasn't the one who screwed things up?" But even he knew he didn't sound very convincing. Which pissed him off.

"Again. I know everything."

"I told you. It just didn't work out." Yeah, if only it were that fucking easy. He glanced back at the closed door. Zoe would be getting madder by the second at being kept waiting. This wasn't his day with women. First Emma, then Zoe, now Beth. "I've gotta go."

"Chase, listen to me." Beth's voice turned low, urgent. "That woman loves you, really *loves* you. I saw it in her eyes. And you don't even want to know what I saw in yours, but I'll tell you, anyway. It was the same thing."

He really, really hated it when Beth was right and the last thing he wanted to think about was what had been in Emma's eyes. Or his. "Beth, stay out of it," he warned.

"The hell I will!" She groaned. "Great. Now you have me swearing in front of the baby. Her first word will probably be *hell* and it will be all your fault."

Chase pulled his mouth tight. He had no response. Nothing.

"Go after her," Beth said. "If you don't, you'll regret it. Shit happens. Get over it. When two people are supposed to be together, like you and Emma are, it's what happens after that matters." She paused. "Kiss the girl. Then tell me I'm wrong and you can live just fine without her."

He wouldn't be able to. And Beth knew it.

"Now I have a baby to feed. Goodbye." *Click.*

Chase jammed the phone back into the pocket of his jeans. Then he balled his hand into a fist again and hit it against the wall. Hard. He heard a picture frame on the other side rattle and jump and winced as his hand reacted in pain. He tried to shake it off, not that it helped.

He'd regret it, she'd said. Yeah, well, who didn't have something they regretted? Didn't change anything.

He'd never felt so helpless, confused, or plain fucking stupid, in his life.

CHAPTER TWENTY

Emma sat in a chair in the corner of her home office, her knees pulled up to her chin, gripping the piece of paper with Madame Claire's phone number written on it. She had opened and closed it so many times, a crease had worn in the middle of it.

Should she call? Ask for the spell to be reversed? If it that happened, everything would go back to the way it had been. Chase would have his successful songwriting career and Emma would be free of Jason Jeffries and his contract.

She could pick herself up from the job layoff and start writing again. Somehow, she would have to know that she really could do it...wouldn't she?

She covered her head with her arms. A hiccup escaped her, the one that was holding back tears she would not allow to fall. The time for tears had passed.

Her do-over hadn't gone as she'd expected. She'd been focused on one thing: another chance with Chase. She'd had that and along with it, moments of pure bliss and pure despair. She'd only hoped for the former, but maybe the kind of love they'd shared couldn't go as deeply as it had without bumps, potholes, and boulders. Otherwise, it would only skim the surface, good enough but never a heart-pounding, soul-melding, forever kind of good.

A lot of good this brilliant revelation does me now. Maybe she could make millions writing a self-help book. *When a Good Do-Over Goes Bad. By Emma Zane, Do-over...ee.*

She sighed, feeling completely and utterly sorry for herself. That lasted for about two minutes before she shook it off, took a deep breath, and told herself to get the hell over it. This was her life and she'd probably overdone the drama on her do-over, anyway.

There had to be something good that had come of this. Or would. She tapped a finger to her chin, thinking. Smaller jeans size. *Nice.* CMA award. *Even nicer.* Bought her mom a house and talked her out of dating loser men. *Touchdown.*

In fact, now that she thought about it, she realized that she'd found something pretty damn good. She'd found Emma again. Or maybe met the *real* Emma for the first time.

The Emma that could latch onto successes, instead of being afraid they'd disappear. The one who didn't let people like Jason Jeffries trample all over her. The Emma who could allow herself enough vulnerability to fully embrace the passion of a night with Chase, no matter what the ultimate outcome. The one who could stand up to her mother and get over her childhood long enough to build something amazing for them both.

And now that she reflected on it, this Emma had discovered she didn't have to trust someone else, she only had to trust *herself* enough to be able to take chances. She might not be all the way there with that one yet, but she was making progress.

Sure, she'd always have to squirrel money away in the bank, but she'd already proven she could work a job without guaranteed hours and pay and know that somehow, some way she'd make it.

This wasn't the old insecure Emma or the new demanding Emma, but a different person entirely, one who could stand firm and still be kind. One who could take a risk if it made sense.

One who could love freely, without requiring an anchor.

Her entire body felt lighter, as though a crushing weight, one that had been with her so long she hadn't even noticed it any more, had been lifted.

She liked this Emma. She didn't want to lose this Emma.

So a do-over of her do-over? *No way.*

It had pierced her heart to see Chase today, to have them not know what to say to each other and end up being overly polite, with subtext running around and over them. It had hurt, but at least she could feel the hurt.

That had to count for something.

Slowly, she uncurled herself, got up, and walked to a small table topped with a fig-and-coconut-scented candle. A book of matches lay beside it. She lit a match and then the wick, watching it flutter and come to life. She blew out the match.

Next, she held up the piece of paper with Madame Claire's phone number. For several seconds, she hesitated as a contentious debate raged inside her, but then she jerked her hand forward to touch the corner of the paper to the flame.

It caught and she held it as it started to burn. When it was nearly consumed, she let the remains fall into the candle, where they turned to ashes. Gone forever.

She would not turn back. She would not *look* back. This was her life now, for better or for worse.

Shoulders straight and chin lifted, she headed to the chair and back to work on the lyrics that she would only ever share with one person. Chase. If he didn't want to see them, she'd be crushed.

But she'd live.

***

Emma's eyes flew open and the pencil rolled from her hand to land with a clatter on the wood floor. Something had awakened her. A sound. There it was again. Loud and insistent, coming from her front door.

She scrambled to her feet, in the process tripping over the fuzzy blanket she'd covered herself with, despite the fact that the central air was desperately trying to cool the house. "Ow." She rubbed at her knee, which had made contact with the wood floor.

More knocking. She got to her feet, hoping against hope it wouldn't be Jason. She had a feeling they would be better off with a long-distance partnership. While living in the same town.

She limped toward the door, rubbing her knee. She opened it to find Chase standing on her doorstep, his jaw set, his gaze locked on her.

Her heart soared, followed just as quickly by a death spiral. She didn't know why he was here, but he didn't look about to gather her in his arms and ride off on a white horse.

Stop it, she told herself. *You've got this, remember?*

He smoothed his t-shirt, as though he didn't know what else to do with his hands, and asked, "Can I come in?"

The resolve she'd felt earlier—at being fine with whatever happened between them—now wasn't anywhere near so resolved. She looked down to give herself a few seconds to think and blew her cheeks out, swallowing the air. She couldn't think, couldn't process. "Um...sure." She took a step back.

He followed her inside to stand in the middle of the room, his thumbs hooked into his jeans.

She closed the door and crossed her arms over her chest. She looked all around the room before finally turning her eyes on him. "How did you find me?"

"I asked. At the label's offices."

"Oh." She motioned toward the sofa. "Sit down." Hopefully he hadn't noticed the tremble in her voice. *Get a grip, Emma.*

"Can't." He didn't. "Beth and Carl had their baby."

"That's great news." Emma clasped her hands in front of her. "Boy or girl?"

"Girl. They named her—" He paused, drawing his brows together. "Leah." He said the baby's name as though relieved he had remembered.

"How's Beth? How big is the baby?"

"Beth's fine. I don't know how big the baby is; I didn't ask." Consternation flitted across his face but then disappeared. "She has hair, though."

"Oh. Hair, that's good." Emma nodded.

He stared at the toe of his boot. She stared at the fireplace. When they spoke again, it was at the same time.

"So you're—," she began.

"Are you—" he said.

Sheepish grins.

"You first," he said.

"No, you." She changed her mind. "Did you come here to tell me about the baby?"

"No. Well, yes, but—" He exhaled. "Can I sit down?"

"Yes."

He took a step toward the sofa, but a few seconds later, moved back to stand close to her.

"How in the hell could you get engaged to someone like that?" he demanded.

"I told you. I'm not."

"Not *anymore.*"

This was a tough one to explain. Madame Claire's voice rang in her mind. *Don't tell anyone or all will unravel most unpredictably.* If that meant what had already happened was "predictable," she didn't even want to contemplate the opposite.

"I wasn't myself." True enough, and it would have to suffice.

"But you sleep with me, let me think—" He broke off to tear at his hair. "And you didn't think it was important to mention you're engaged to somebody else."

Chase had a clear moral code; it was one of the things she loved most about him. "It was wrong," she said simply. "*I* was wrong."

Again, he raked his hand through his hair. At this rate, he wouldn't have any left. "Of all the guys to say you'd marry, it had to be that asshole." His nostrils flared and he began to pace across the room. "It wasn't enough what happened before, you had to get back with him again."

"I know you're going to have trouble believing this, but it wasn't that way. It wasn't." Her hands flailed helplessly. "I wasn't really *with* him. And I don't even remember him proposing, let alone me saying yes. He was the one who told me we were engaged. I never did have a ring."

"Only because he would want his publicist to make the announcement." His tone was dry, close to mocking.

"Fine. Probably." She was beginning to get angry now, but she didn't know if it was because she felt horribly misunderstood or because she was upset with herself for all the same reasons he had. Her fingernails pressed hard into her palms.

"Another thing. Did you come looking for me because you wanted help writing songs?"

It would be easy to deny it, but maybe on some level, she had. "I don't know," she admitted. She crossed the room, sat carefully on the sofa, and looked up at him. "But would that be such a bad thing?"

He rubbed his forehead and blinked at her. "What?"

She repeated the question. "If I had wanted to write with you again, would that be such a bad thing?"

"That's not the point."

"You brought it up."

"I—I don't even know what the point is, anymore."

"Of this conversation? Or of us?" *Don't say us, please don't say us.*

Chase looked up at the ceiling and closed his eyes. "I felt like shit when you saw me with Zoe today. It felt like I was cheating or something, which doesn't make any sense because you and I haven't written together for years. And you're the one who *actually* cheated. On me, with me."

She inhaled deeply. "You can write with whoever you want to. You and Zoe would make a good team." Dagger to the heart. She hated that woman.

"You wouldn't have felt like that if I'd written something with her back…then." His last word stumbled and fell.

"I'm sure you're right, but that was a long time ago." Her voice was soft, thinking back. It was as if she had been wearing sunglasses and had just taken them off, squinting at the brightness, but willing to trade that for how much clearer everything looked. "But you didn't write with someone else."

She lay back against the sofa and looked up at him, into his eyes. "I don't think you were as mad as I thought you were about the money part of selling the lyrics, though I didn't realize it at the time."

He tipped his chin, mouth pulled tight.

"It was about me selling out on our dream, the one we made together," she went on. "About me as good as telling you I didn't believe we could ever get there, that we could do it. Instead of telling you how I felt, how scared I was, I gave up on us." She shook her head. "It was easier that way."

"Easier," he repeated.

Her thoughts raced, taking the turns at breakneck speed. "Jason shouldn't have told you about it. You shouldn't have had to find out that way, in the bar. I can't apologize for him, but I know I should have told you before he did. That wasn't right, and I'm sorry."

"You're sorry." Neither of them moved. All around them went still and quiet, waiting. Then Chase said, "This won't work, Emma. I don't know why I'm here."

He turned and strode away, the heels of his boots ringing on the wooden floor. She heard the door close behind him.

Again, *again* the love of her life had walked out. Her muscles began quivering and her heartbeat zoomed over the speed limit. She was away from the sofa before she realized it, headed for the front door. She flung it open to see Chase standing at the driver's side of his truck, head down.

She clattered down the steps and had covered the distance between them in seconds. He looked up.

"You *can* do this," she said, hands on her hips. "But you won't. Because your head's too hard."

His brows drew into a V. "Really."

"If you leave right now, you're going to regret it for the rest of your life. And trust me, I know something about regret. You wouldn't like it." Her breath was coming in short, sharp bursts.

He rounded the front of the truck until he was standing just inches from her. "What makes you think I don't have regrets?"

"Then do something about it."

"Oh, I'll do something about it." He pulled her to him, his mouth closing in on hers, hot and hungry. He drew back for a second, their lips clinging. "You want to stand out here or go inside?"

She didn't answer, just began backing up, toward the house. He went with her step for step, his body pressed to hers, his mouth kissing her hard. At the stairs leading to the porch, he stopped moving to scoop her into his arms.

A girl could get used to this kind of thing.

CHAPTER TWENTY-ONE

As he walked into the house with Emma in his arms, Chase didn't break their kiss. He didn't want his mouth to ever leave hers again, unless it was to roam over other parts of her body.

He made a move toward a closed door that looked likely. She made a sound that redirected him to another door. He pushed it open with the toe of his boot.

A wide expanse of bed against the wall awaited them. He laid her down as gently as he could, his breath coming faster, his heart beating so fast it blurred all thought until he focused only on the aching, driving need to have her naked body in his arms.

She peeled off his t-shirt, flinging it somewhere across the room. He did the same with the lacy, flimsy top she had on. In the space of a few seconds, it and her bra had joined his t-shirt, and he had his mouth on her breasts, cupping them with his hands, teasing her nipples with his tongue.

Her hands were on the waistband of his jeans, loosening the button and undoing his zipper. When he felt her fingers brush against his erection, through the cotton of his briefs, he thought for a moment he might go insane. And then all thought suspended again, until he was in a place where he could only feel. With his mouth, his hands, his dick. His heart.

When all clothes had been discarded and they were lying naked on the comforter, he ran his hand from her soft hair, to her cheeks, to her breasts, and down. Then he groaned in anticipation as she pushed him over onto his back. "Let *me*," she said, her voice so husky, his already stiff, aching dick raised its proverbial head to pay attention. *Shit*. This woman had him by the balls. And he was a willing prisoner.

She started out by circling one red fingernail around and around his abdomen, touching everything but its main target until his back arched in aching anticipation. She grasped and began stroking him, long and hard. His eyes were closed tight, but he was pretty sure she was watching him and having one hell of a time enjoying herself.

Then her lips closed on him and he lost the ability to think of anything but the sheer, blinding pleasure that engulfed him. *Emma. Oh God, Emma.*

He reciprocated in kind, relishing her moans and pushing them higher in range and intensity until he was sure his touch, his tongue on her clit, had brought her to a place of searing pleasure, until neither one of them could wait any longer for him to bury his cock inside her tight, warm flesh. For the ultimate high that followed his hard thrusts, where they were joined in one simultaneous, shuddering orgasm.

Wet, spent, and breathing hard, he rolled over, but immediately folded her into his arms, unwilling to be apart from her, even for a few minutes. He kissed her again, long, tender, and strong. They were both gasping for air when they pulled away.

Lying on his back, with the woman he loved in his arms, he decided to address the unfinished business. "I was a jerk. I'm stubborn and my pride…it took a hit and I was mad. I thought—" He balled one fist. "I thought I should never have to share you with anyone. Your talent. Your *you*, the part that only I got to see."

He dared a glance at her. She waited, watching him.

No easy out, then. He was going to have to go on. Not that the confession wasn't long overdue. "And I knew that if you were worried enough about us making it that you sold your lyrics to someone else, you already had one foot out the door back to Seattle. I'd never get you back."

"We made mistakes." Her fingers trailed along his chest, sending a thrill through him. "Everybody does. We were only teenagers."

He closed his eyes to concentrate. "Beth told me something. She said, the way you looked at me, she could tell you still love me." He held his breath. What if she was only looking for closure, for that apology, and then she'd move on?

Emma lifted her chin and met his eyes. "Beth is right."

He cupped her chin with his hand, pulling her closer. His lips hovered barely an inch from hers.

"What else did Beth say?" she breathed.

"She said she could tell I still love you."

"Is she right?"

It wasn't as hard to admit as he'd thought it would be. He nodded, but not enough to break what had them in its grasp. His heart hammered in his chest. "Yes."

"Well, Beth is a professional."

"She is." He put his other hand on her face, on her warm, soft skin.

"Chase…"

"Yes?" he whispered in her ear.

"There's something we need to do. Now."

His dick stirred, ready to be called into action. "I'm ready, love."

"Good." She slid from his arms and from the bed, tossing him his jeans. "You have your guitar?"

"Hold on." He shook his head. "What?"

"Your guitar."

"It's in the truck."

She beckoned to him with her index finger, a slow smile on her face. "Get it."

"Now?"

"Now."

A few minutes later, he'd climbed back into his jeans to retrieve his guitar from the seat of his truck. He didn't know what the hell she had in mind, but at this point, he was all in. When he went back inside, he saw Emma sitting cross-legged on the sofa, wearing only a thin, see-through bra and a thong. Damn, the woman was going to kill him. At least he'd die happy. "You looking for a serenade?" he croaked.

"We have something we need to do. Sit down." She pointed to the seat next to her.

He did as she asked, but leaned in for a kiss, intoxicated by the smell of sex and lavender mingling on her nearly naked body. "Right here?" he asked.

"We're going to finish it. 'Wishsome.' You and me, the way we would have written it together."

He pulled back, pushing through the arousal that had his head spinning and his mind buzzing to make some sense out of this. "'Wishsome' is written. Done." He frowned. What the hell was she doing, bringing that fucking song up now?

She put her hands on either side of his face. "Listen to me. Really listen."

Something inside him calmed at her touch. "I'm listening."

"*We* never finished it. We don't have to do anything with it, ever, in fact we *can't*, but we have to finish it. For us."

"It's that important to you."

"It's that important to me," she agreed. "We meant it to be a ballad, a love song, not the crap that came out on the radio."

He picked up his guitar and laid it across his lap, looping his arm over it. "Okay." He took a deep breath and thought back. Years. "We had started with something like this." He began to play, softly and hesitantly at first.

Emma's pure voice began to sing, high and soulful.

It all starts with a wish
Carries on with a kiss
And the one you've longed for
Is making your heart soar
Tying it up with a twist

He nodded and kept going. They reached the chorus and he stopped, hand leaving the strings. "This is the part we could never get right."

"I know." She also nodded. "So let's try again."

"Are you sure you don't want to instead, you know…" He jerked his head back toward the bedroom. That bra of hers, which hid nothing at all, was doing things to him. Good things.

"Concentrate," she instructed.

"Fine," he sighed. A man had to try.

And so he tried out a few possibilities, screwing his eyes shut and thinking hard about the chorus that should go with this song. After a few different options that didn't go anywhere, he felt Emma's hands on his chest, from behind. She had climbed to his spot on the sofa and had pressed her breasts into his back, her hands stroking his chest, his nipples.

Aw, shit. She was going lower. His dick ached, his thinking clouded.

"Compose," she whispered, her breath tickling his ear. She sidled up further until her breasts were at the tops of his shoulders and her fingers were undoing the button of his waistband, probing beneath. "Emma," he pleaded, his voice not even making a sound.

"You can do it." He felt her lips on his neck, tender kisses that promised more.

He took a shaky breath and began playing again. She undid his zipper and damn near undid him, but he played. And kept playing.

She stopped, pulling away abruptly and scampering back to sit beside him.

His cry of dismay caught in his throat.

"That's it," she said.

He fell back against the sofa, groaning in agony. "Fuck, Emma. What are you trying to do to me?"

"Play it again," she urged. "That's it."

"I can't even remember it."

"Yes, you can. It's like this." She began humming the melody.

He played it again, with all of the aching desire still consuming him.

Emma began to sing.

When you wish some,
Hope some,
Try some
Die some...

He joined in. When they finished the rest of the chorus, he looked at her. And she looked at him. "We did it," he breathed. "That was the part we could never get."

"We did it." The smile on her face was so big it could have powered all of Nashville on its own.

"Time to celebrate." He scooped her into his arms, reveling in the feel of her body against his chest.

"Wait!"

Alarm shot through him. "What is it?"

"You haven't had any—chili beans, have you?"

Oh, crap. He set her down, cupped his palm and blew into it, panicking that he'd blown it. "No. Why, do you smell chili?"

"No." She shook her head. "I just had to be sure."

"Of what?"

She laughed, tugging on his hand. "That the end doesn't justify the beans. That the only love spell you're under is *mine.*"

He shook his head, baffled. "I don't get it."

"Someday, I might tell you. But for now, it's nothing. Just—never mind."

She reached up to kiss him, pressing her breasts into his chest, and he forgot whatever it was they'd been talking about. Beth was right. That kiss told him everything; he never wanted to again live without Emma in his life.

"Say it," she urged. "I want to hear it. I've been waiting to hear it."

"I love you." His mouth touched hers. "I do. I love you."

When they came up for air, he said, "Now you say it."

"I love you," she whispered. "I always have."

"We finally finished the song."

"Yes, we did."

"And we're done with apologies."

"Done," she agreed. "Now, would you like to go back to bed?"

He chuckled. "More than anything."

***

The mid-spring day was an unseasonably warm one, with flowers spreading across the landscape in a riot of joyful color and the grasses green and lush.

Maven, Ohio was ready for a celebration.

Emma huddled in one of the Chapman farmhouse's newly renovated bedrooms with her mother, who was resplendent in a chic grey dress with pearls at her neck, her matron of honor, Beth, and her tiny flower girl, ten-month-old Leah, who would be riding down the aisle in a flower-strewn wagon. Lila the dog would be following close behind, with tiny roses on her collar and in her mouth, the handles of a basket holding the rings.

Beth, already dressed in her strapless long satin and crepe dress, was preoccupied with keeping Leah out of the flower bouquets. "We have to put them up out of her reach," she said, looking for a suitable place.

"Have you seen him yet?" Emma asked the room in general. Whoever answered, her mom, Beth or Leah, was fine. She just wanted to know.

"I have," her mother announced. "He looks very handsome, sweetheart."

Emma beamed. She didn't think her heart could get any fuller than this.

A knock at the door and Carl poked his head in.

"Carl!" Beth scolded. "I said you couldn't come in here."

He raised his hand to show the video camera he clasped. "It's okay. I'm not the groom."

"The ceremony, Carl," Beth reminded him. "That's what you can tape. And the reception. That's all."

"Fine," he answered grudgingly. "I just wanted to get the whole experience. This is going to be great on the web site. The first Matches Made in Maven wedding. Man, it's a good day."

Beth shook her head, smiling. "It's a good day, but business isn't the important part. Now get out of here." She made shooing gestures with her hands and rushed to grab her speed-crawling daughter, who was determined to go under the bed.

"It *is* a good day," Emma smiled, gazing out the window in back of the house, where white chairs and a handmade altar had been set up, decorated with an abundance of flowers and ribbons in pale pink and ivory. "It's a *wonderful* day." Her assistant, Taryn, was directing the rolling of a runner down the center aisle, adjusting it every few feet to ensure it remained straight.

Emma had expected to feel some last-minute anxiety over the wedding details, but instead, she'd never felt so calm, so at peace. She was marrying the man she loved more than anything or anyone and all was right with the world.

She turned to her mother. "Is Lacey here yet?"

"I'm sure she is. I'll just step out and check."

"You'll be able to tell right away. Lacey can't help but make an entrance wherever she goes." Emma laughed softly.

Lacey Simpson, a popular new country singer, had recorded Chase and Emma's song, "Heart Pine Beams," which had just reached number two on the charts. They'd hoped for number one by the day of the wedding, but they'd take two. Lacey had done the song proud. And she was going to sing it, accompanied by Carl's band, for Chase and Emma's first dance at the reception.

Trina Zane came back into the room, followed by Taryn, who closed the door behind them. "Lacey's here. And it's nearly time," Trina said, beaming. "Let's get you into your dress."

With the help of the other three women, Emma slipped into her strapless ivory wedding dress. The lace bodice had a delicate peplum that floated above a full skirt of tulle and organza. It was classic and elegant and she had fallen for it the moment she'd tried it on.

Minutes later, she stood at the end of the cloth runner as the string quartet concluded its music for the seating and began playing

Pachelbel's "Canon in D." The pastor signaled to the guests, who all stood and turned toward Emma.

With the sun kissing her bare shoulders, she clutched her bouquet of roses and began walking slowly toward Chase, her dress swishing softly around her. He looked more handsome than she had ever seen him, in a tux perfectly fitted to his tall, lean body and a single pale rose, its edges tipped in pink, in his lapel.

She smiled from side to side, greeting friends, but her attention was focused only on Chase—on his crooked smile, the bits of his hair that refused to behave as told, and the fact that she wanted to run down the aisle and jump into his arms, instead of doing this slow wedding walk.

When she reached him at last, she grabbed his hand and squeezed tight, loving the way he put her hand to his heart and how the corners of his eyes crinkled.

Just over his shoulder, Emma caught sight of a familiar figure. It would have been hard to miss her. Madame Claire was seated on the bride's side, wearing a dark purple dress and pale orange hair, and nodding her approval with an expression that crept dangerously close to a smile.

Though this do-over had begun in a slightly terrifying way, Emma decided, in the end, all was as it should be. Emma winked at her fairy godpsychic and received an answering wink in return, though it appeared as though it might have pained the woman to move her face that way.

The next thing she knew, the pastor was pronouncing her and Chase husband and wife. They looked at each other, counted silently to three, and sent a roaring "Yee-haw!" up to the heavens. Then they half danced, half floated down the aisle and headed for the newly restored barn, where they would greet their guests and dance all night to the music of Carl's band.

It was a magical sight, the barn transformed with hundreds of white lights and overflowing baskets of flowers. Chase had created a dance floor especially for the occasion, and along one wall, tables covered with ivory linen were heaped with food watched over by caterers dressed in black.

Emma laughed, hugged and grinned through the reception line, never moving more than an inch from her new husband. It seemed that most of Maven had turned out for the wedding, including Chrissy and her mother, who was proudly sporting a snowman pin.

The last person in line was a tall, strikingly beautiful woman Emma had never seen. She had the kind of bone structure women envied, straight, shiny hair, and a body that would turn heads at a conference of supermodels. Chase introduced her as his cousin, from L.A. "This is Anya," he said, giving her a hug. "It's been too long since we've seen each other."

Anya kept her chin down, but gave Emma a shy smile. "What a lovely wedding," she said. "I'm very happy for you both."

Emma beamed. "Thank you for coming. I'm glad to meet you."

"Tell me how everything is in L.A.," Chase said, leading Anya away. "Your parents couldn't come?"

Beth stepped up to Emma's ear to whisper, "Cross your fingers for another Match Made in Maven."

"Anya's a client of yours? That fast? Wow, I would think she could date anyone she wanted. She's gorgeous."

"Not from what I understand," Beth said with a sympathetic cluck of her tongue. "Chase's father told me she hasn't been the same since the accident."

It never ceased to amaze Emma how much Beth learned about people in a short amount of time. Beth had told Emma she just had one of those faces that caused people to tell her things. Personal things.

"Not sure what happened," Beth continued, "but she ended up with a scar she's pretty self-conscious about."

"I didn't notice."

"She keeps her hair over it. I don't think it's such a big deal, though."

"If there's true love to be found, you'll help her find it. In Ohio, though? Or are you telling me you're opening a field office in L.A.?"

"Maybe someday." Beth's eyes twinkled. "She's not exactly a client yet, but who knows what could happen?" Her manner turned brisk, all business. "I was, after all, pretty successful with Angela's sister from Athens." She pointed at a pretty young woman, who waved, the ring on her third finger sparkling in the sunlight.

Angela's sister from Athens. Emma looked at the woman in a new light, realizing just how close Chase had come to being set up with the woman. By Beth. "Glad I got to him first," she murmured.

Beth tipped her head, questioning.

"Nothing," Emma said hurriedly. "Oh, look! It's time for our first dance."

Chase's father had stepped up to the microphone to, as Chase and Emma had requested, introduce Lacey Simpson. The country singer rained her sunshine persona down on the assembled guests and began to sing "Heart Pine Beams," accompanied by Carl's band.

Emma's words, capturing a love as enduring as the architecturally beautiful, strong beams supporting the two-hundred-year-old house she'd restored in Nashville, set to Chase's music. Chase folded her tenderly in his arms and they swayed on the dance floor together in perfect rhythm.

She kissed her husband, luxuriating in the taste, the feel of his lips on hers. Then she peeked around his shoulder until her eyes landed on the woman who had, along with Emma, had enough courage not to listen to her dead mother's recommendation.

Madame Claire didn't see her, though. Because she was deep in conversation at a table with Anya, Chase's cousin.

"Happy?" Chase whispered in her ear as the song drew to its soaring conclusion.

"Better than happy," Emma replied. "I can't even find the words to describe how I feel."

"What?" He drew back in mock horror. "Songwriter of the Year and words fail you?"

"Sometimes…" she said, one eyebrow sky high, "you don't need words." Then she kissed him again, to show him why.

THE END

ABOUT THE AUTHOR

A native of the Pacific Northwest, Jane and her family recently moved to Ohio. She loves reading and writing books with feel-good endings, rescuing dogs in need of a home, feeding a shameless addiction to both reality TV and PBS, exploring the country with her husband, and being a mom.

She is also the author of *Grab the Brass Ring*, *Say It Again, Sam*, and *Be Careful What You Kiss For.*

Did you enjoy this book? Drop us a line and say so! We love to hear from readers, and so do our authors. To connect, visit www.boroughspublishinggroup.com online, send comments directly to info@boroughspublishinggroup.com, or friend us on Facebook and Twitter. And be sure to check back regularly for contests and new releases in your favorite subgenres of romance!

Are you an aspiring writer? Check out www.boroughspublishinggroup.com/submit and see if we can help you make your dreams come true.